Rosa

Not just hot...

SCARY HOT

AN UNTIL SERIES AND CLUB ALIAS SERIES
CROSSOVER

KD ROBICHAUX

XOXO

KD Robichaux

Cover by Pink Ink Designs
Edited by Barb Hoover at Hot Tree Editing

CONTENTS

ALSO BY KD ROBICHAUX

THE BLOGGER DIARIES TRILOGY

Wished for You (FREE)

Wish He Was You

Wish Come True

The Blogger Diaries Trilogy Boxed Set (Special Price)

CLUB ALIAS SERIES (Available in KU)

Book 1/ *Confession Duet Boxed Set:*

Before the Lie

Truth Revealed

Book 2/ *Seven: A Club Alias Novel*

Book 2.5/ *Mission: Accomplished Novella Boxed Set*

Book 3/ *Knight: A Club Alias Novel*

Book 3.5/ *Scary Hot* (Until and Club Alias Crossover)

STANDALONES

No Trespassing

Steal You

COMING SOON

Doc: A Club Alias Novel

PREFACE

Kayan and Z are the best friends in Aurora Rose Reynolds's Until July. I fell in love with them and couldn't wait to give them a book of their own. Scary Hot is completely standalone, so don't worry if you've never met them before.

Thank you, Aurora, for giving me the opportunity to let these wonderful characters take over my imagination and become mine for just a little while.

~KD

1

KAYAN

I wake with a start, gasping as I sit up at the sound of LeFou barking his little face off from his crate in the living room. What the heck? He's pretty quiet at night, aside from his compulsive licking—hence why he doesn't sleep in bed with me. So what in the world is the little guy freaking out about?

There's a short lull in the high-pitched yapping as the Chihuahua catches his breath, in which I hear movement and a muffled thud—my window shutting?—before his barking continues, more frantic this time.

I shake off my grogginess. I had just gone to sleep after peeling myself out of one of the sweet black catsuits July —my business partner-slash-BFF—and I wore on our stakeout. With all the excitement of the night, I'd fallen asleep before my head hit the pillow. Reaching into the middle drawer of my nightstand, I pull out my .38 revolver, silently standing in my bare feet as my heart thuds inside my ribcage. I pull the hammer back slowly, as quietly as I can, the weapon feeling comfortable in my capable hands.

A membership at the local shooting range, which I visit three times a week to blow off steam using paper targets, insures I'm a damn good shot and not squeamish around my handgun, one I've owned for several years but have luckily never had to use in a real life situation.

Between LeFou's incessant yapping, I hear the floor-boards in my living room creek, and I press my back to the wall beside my bedroom door. Carefully, I look around the doorjamb, peeking down the hall of my apartment to see if I can spot whatever is causing my dog to bark.

There, beside my couch dimly lit only by the moon-light shining in through the windows, is a hulking figure. I hold back a gasp, my heart picking up its pace as I take in the sheer size of whoever is in my apartment uninvited.

Is this one of the guys Wes was warning July and me about? Is this why he got so pissed we went on our stakeout and followed the guy to Momma's Country bar? I mean, what did he expect us to do? We finally caught whoever it was leaving those fighting dogs at our vet clinic. Surely he didn't think we *wouldn't* follow him? We had questions. We wanted to know who it was fighting the poor creatures so we could stop them. We also wanted to know why he kept bringing them to us when it was already too late for most of them.

"Shut the fuck up," comes the deep voice I barely make out over my pulse in my ears, and to my surprise, LeFou stops barking.

I frown. Nobody talks to my freaking dog like that. Poor fella had been through enough in his hard little life before I adopted him from our clinic. No stupid intruder is going to hurt his feelings, my protective, noble, little steed.

I step out into my hallway, raise my gun to aim at his head, but at the last minute, I aim lower and to the right, squeezing the trigger. With my adrenaline pumping and my heart beating so loudly, the gun going off barely makes me flinch. Neither does the grunt that leaves the giant man's throat as he stumbles backward at the shot to his shoulder.

"Kitten." The intruder sounds... hurt? Betrayed? And why the hell did he say—

Oh no.

Oh no no no no no.

I slap my arm against the wall of the hallway and swish my hand around until my finger catches the light switch, and I flip it upward. When light fills the small room, my jaw drops as I take in Z's tall body taking up most of the space in my living room. He immediately looks down at his shoulder, then turns to glance behind him. My eyes follow the direction in which he's looking, and I see the bullet must've gone straight through and imbedded in my wall. Thank goodness no one lives in the other half of my duplex and I don't have neighbors for miles. I won't have to worry about someone calling the cops about a gunshot— Oh shit.

"Oh shit!" I start to panic, rushing toward Z. "Oh my God, I shot you! Now I'm gonna go to jail. I won't survive jail! Look at me!" I gesture to my small yet curvy body with my revolver, forgetting it was in my hand.

When his eyes roam over me, heat instantly filling

them as he pulls his full bottom lip between his teeth, I glance down at myself.

Naked.

Of course I'm naked. Those catsuits left nothing to the imagination and you could see every nook, cranny, and bump. Not even Spanx would've worked underneath, because you could've seen where the spandex stopped around your ribs and thighs. So I went au naturel, and only took the time to strip before collapsing in bed.

His deep voice rumbles throughout my apartment and directly through the nerves connecting my nipples to my clit, making both throb, awakening with desire. "Shy little kitten knows her way around a gun. Makes me wonder if it's only the metal kind, or if she can handle the flesh and blood kind."

I gasp at his words, stepping back inside my bedroom doorway. I place my gun on my dresser, yanking open the drawer to pull out one of my Soma nightshirts. I always thought it was an old lady brand... until I felt the soft material against my skin. I'd gotten rid of every pajama I owned and replaced them with these in every color and pattern they made.

Oh, God. Z was going to see me in my old lady nightgown!

Wait a second.

Why am I embarrassed more by that thought than a moment ago when he saw me naked?

Z is not just hot. He's *scary* hot.

Hot, I can handle like a champ. I can make hot bend to my will and worship the ground I walk on. But *scary* hot? Brings out a submissive side of me I'm not 100 percent sure I like.

Taking a deep breath and letting it out, I step back out into the hallway, my brow furrowing when I see Z is no longer in my living room. Peeking around the wall, relief fills me when I see he's in my kitchen, standing hunched over my sink with the water running. I would've been in complete panic if he had left, thinking he was on his way to the hospital and then to rat me out.

But he was the one who broke into my house! It was self-defense! Or protecting my property... or something.

With that thought in mind, I go to ask him what the hell he was doing sneaking in through my window, but what comes out is, "Are you okay? I'm so sorry." My lip trembles, remembering the hurt in his voice after I shot him.

His eyes come to me when I step near him to get a closer look, his face softening when he sees my regret. "It's all right. Nothing I haven't been through before." My eyes widen in shock, but before I can ask what he means, he asks, "Do you have any needle and thread? Bullet went straight through."

"Um... no. I'm not that domestic." I blush.

"Aren't you a vet tech or something?" he asks, tilting his head.

"No." I shake my head. "I'm an office manager. I majored in Business Management while July went to veterinary school so we could open up our own clinic."

I can almost see the idea form in his head as soon as my best friend's name leaves my lips. He reaches for his pocket, for his phone I assume, but I grab his hand, electricity instantly zinging where our flesh touches. "Please. Don't tell her I shot you. She'd never let me live it down."

"She not okay with guns?" He lifts a sexy brow. How can a man's eyebrows be sexy?

I shake my head. "No, it's not that. She just doesn't like me living alone. She's offered several times for me to move in with her, but I like my space. Plus, working with someone every day and then also living with them... seemed like way too much time spent with one person."

He gives a short nod before pulling out his phone. He scrolls, finds the name he's looking for, and then lifts the cell to his ear. "Hey, man. Need you to come pick me up and take me to your vet. I've been shot."

Wes says something, and Z's eyes meet mine. "Yep, the little kitten apparently has claws. But let's keep that between us, yeah?" Wes must agree, because Z winks at me and gives another little nod. "I'll text you the address."

My eyes narrow at that, which causes him to smirk as he tells Wes bye and hangs up. "You have my address memorized? How did you even find where I live anyway?" I inquire.

"Former military, babe. I have my ways. And I had to scope out the area just in case," he tells me, pulling out a couple drawers then looking on top of my refrigerator. "Where do you keep your kitchen towels?"

"Under the sink," I reply. "But scope out the area just in case of what?" I feel like a parrot, repeating his words, but he's so vague I need clarification.

"In case of anything," he answers just as vaguely, and I roll my eyes. It's obvious he's just as unforthcoming as Wes is with July. He reaches beneath the sink and pulls out a couple of dishtowels. "You have any duct tape?"

His non-answer irks me enough that I forget for a split second he's trying to take care of his gunshot wound, the gunshot wound *I* put in his shoulder. "Do I look like the type of woman who owns duct tape?" I ask sassily, popping my hip.

"Well... you're the type of woman who has damn good aim with the handgun she clearly knows how to use properly, so by that alone, yes. You look like you could be prepared for just about anything." He smiles sexily, making my toes curl against my cold kitchen floor.

I give in. "Ugh. You're right. Drawer under the microwave." I'd get it for him, but his big body is blocking it. When he pulls it out and sets it on the counter then begins to struggle trying to hold the dishtowels to his shoulder, I finally jump into action. "Here. Sit down at the table." I tug his arm gently toward one of the chairs. I'm worried the legs on it might snap he looks so large as he lowers himself into it, but when he stays upright, I set to work.

Grabbing some scissors from a drawer, I cut off the short sleeve of his black tee he's wearing under his leather biker vest with all its patches. I vaguely remember it being called a "cut" after binge-watching *Sons of Anarchy*. The bullet went straight through, so I have him hold one folded towel to the front of his shoulder while I hold one to the back before grabbing the end of the tape with my teeth. But I stop, thinking twice.

"Hold that thought," I tell him, setting the tape down on the table before quickly disappearing into my bedroom. "Shit." Realizing I can't use one of my belts, because I wear super blingy ones that July would recognize in a heartbeat, I hurry back to Z. "Stand up a sec," I say, and he cocks his head to the side with a small smile before doing as I requested.

Without much thought, I reach for his waist, lifting his black t-shirt to reveal that he is in fact wearing a black leather belt... and a tiny bit of his rippled, tan stomach that has a soft-looking patch of hair leading from his belly button down into his jeans. Gulping, my hands tremble as I unhook his belt, way too much of a chicken shit to look up into his ruggedly handsome face when I pull it from the loops.

My voice is quiet when I ask him to sit back down, adding, "Duct tape on armpit hair seemed like a bad idea on top of being shot. I think I've tortured you enough for one evening."

"Not even close." His voice is a cross between a growl and a purr, way too sexy for my lady bits to ignore, and I can't help but meet his eyes. There's a shit load of heat there, along with a silent question I don't understand. What are those dark chocolate eyes asking me?

Deciding not to respond so I don't embarrass myself, I put my dishtowel back into place and wrap his belt tightly around his arm. His shoulder and bicep are so huge the belt actually fastens through one of the holes, making it easy to keep it in place. I hurry over to my kitchen counter, pulling off a bunch of paper towels and wetting them before returning to Z's side. I clean up the blood that had dripped down his arm since he rinsed it in my sink and check the makeshift tourniquet, thankful when I see I've made it tight enough that no more blood is oozing from the wound.

"That should get you to July's house," I tell him. "Again, I'm so so—"

"I'm fine, kitten. It's actually kinda a relief," he interrupts, making my brows furrow in confusion.

"Quit calling me that. My name is Kayan. As in Kay-Anne. Not cayenne. And definitely not kitten. Now, how could being shot be a relief?" I question.

He ignores my griping. "Means you aren't this helpless little thing that needs constant protection. You're not the damsel in distress your tiny, delicious little body makes you appear," he rumbles, and my face flushes.

"I told you before I don't need to be protected," I whisper shyly, unable to make my voice any louder, and I watch his eyes twinkle.

"You're as shy as a kitten. Don't think I've ever had shy in my bed." His words from when I ran into him at Momma's Country fill my mind, sending a tickle through my belly.

Before either of us can speak, there's a knock at my door, snapping me out of my Z-induced haze. "Must be Wes," I say, and hurry over to let him in. When I open the door, the words rush out of my mouth. "It's not my fault. He crawled in through my window while I was sleeping, and my dog—" I gesture toward LeFou's crate, seeing the little creature has curled himself into his blankets and gone back to sleep. "—was freaking the hell out. I didn't know it was him! Please don't tell July."

"I won't tell July," he promises with a soft smile and a pat to my shoulder as he walks past me to Z. "How long did ya make it this time, old friend?" He grins at his biker brother.

"Name's Z, and before tonight, I hadn't been shot in two hundred and twenty-one days," he jokes as if he's introducing himself at an Alcoholics Anonymous meeting. Both of them glance at me when I gasp, and I shake my head.

"How can y'all be joking about something like this?

And it's a *running* joke? How many times have you been shot?" My voice rises in pitch with each question until it's squeaky and loud.

Z chuckles, making my nipples peak. "This makes lucky number seven, kitten."

My knees almost buckle. "You've been shot seven times? And you're *alive*?"

"Not all at once." He shrugs his uninjured shoulder nonchalantly.

I can't take any more mind-boggling revelations from these two. Suddenly feeling exhausted, my adrenaline probably waning, I tell him, "Well, again, sorry for shooting you. Hopefully you've learned your lesson about sneaking in through people's windows. I'm going to bed."

Wes stands by as Z lifts himself out of the dwarfed dining chair, reaching out to steady Z when he wobbles slightly. Concern fills my chest, but I force myself to continue on to my bedroom.

2

Z

"**O**pen up!" Wes shouts, banging on July's door.

"Bro, chill. You're gonna scare the poor thing," I tell him, my uninjured arm around Wes's shoulders, since the blood loss is definitely getting to me.

"What's going on?" July asks sleepily when she opens the door.

"He got shot," Wes tells her, and July's eyes come to me then go round as saucers when she sees blood soaking through Kayan's kitchen towels strapped there.

"You need to go to the hospital," she squeaks.

"Can't," he says shortly.

"Wes, I'm a vet, not a doctor."

"Jesus," I grumble, my head swimming, and Wes gently moves July out of the way as he walks us into the house and helps me get seated in one of her white kitchen chairs that creaks under my weight.

"Baby." Wes turns and stands in front of her, his palms gently going to her cheeks to make her eyes focus on his and not me. "I need you to help him. The wound is clean through, so all you need to do is sew it up."

"Wes," I hear her whisper, and she peers around him to peek at me.

"Look at me." His voice raises, and I see him lower his face toward hers. "I need your help, baby."

She seems to search his face before she finally whispers, "Okay," then she clears her throat. "I need to go to the clinic and get supplies. I don't have anything here."

"I'll take you," Wes tells her.

"No, you stay with him. I'll go and be back quickly." She goes to what I assume is her bedroom, because when she returns, she's wearing a pair of jeans, a sweatshirt, and tennis shoes. She walks past us and heads out to what I see is her garage when she opens the door, immediately noticing she's blocked in by Wes's SUV.

"I'm driving you," Wes says, stepping out into the garage. He gives me a chin lift before closing the door behind them.

The house is too quiet after they leave, so I stand, holding onto the table and then the countertops as I open her refrigerator, looking for something to drink. Nothing, not even beer. So I rummage through her cabinets, sighing a "Thank fuck" when I discover a dusty bottle of Jack.

I ease myself back onto the chair, swiping the dust off the bottle before unscrewing the cap and lifting it to my lips for a swig, breathing out as I think about the past half hour. I can't help the smile that tugs at my mouth, thinking about the tiny woman who shot me.

You couldn't have paid me to believe that Kayan not only knew how to shoot, but owned her own gun to protect herself with. And not some pussy-ass gun neither, like a .22 or some shit. A .38 revolver she held straight and steady. Before I could move out of the way, stunned into freezing my position in her living room at the sight of her naked form pointing a gun at me, I saw the split-second decision she made to move her aim from my head to my shoulder. I have no doubt I would be dead right now without her last-minute change of heart, because her aim was true. I'd have to have a talk with her about that. If it were anyone else, she'd either need to shoot them dead or choose somewhere more debilitating than a shoulder, so the intruder wouldn't be able to come after her like I easily could have.

Thinking of her perfect naked body, my cock swells inside my jeans, and I reach down to adjust it, the movement making the dining chair creak once again. I can't remember the last time a woman affected me the way Kayan does, if ever. It was an instant attraction. No, not just an attraction. A *connection*. As soon as I looked into her gorgeous eyes, everything inside me growled, "*Mine*."

Just then, July and Wes arrive, and seeing the bag of tools in her hand, I shake my head. "You better not neuter me, girl." I smile, trying to ease some of the anxiety I see written over her face.

"You probably need to be neutered," she replies, and I grin before eying the stuff she sets out on the table. "Can I ask how this happened?" she asks softly, pulling the belt loose and the towels away from my shoulder and looking at the wound.

"No," Wes inserts before I can, pulling out a chair and taking a seat across the table from me.

"You don't think I have the right to know, when you

show up at my house in the early hours of the morning, asking me to stitch up a guy with a gunshot wound, while refusing to take him to the hospital?" She narrows her eyes on him, and he doesn't even flinch.

"Nothing you need to worry about." He looks at me, assuring me with his eyes that he's not going to rat out my girl.

My girl. I smile to myself over the fact I'm thinking of her that way when I barely know her. Not to mention she just shot me.

Wes's answer clearly pisses July off. She pours some alcohol onto a piece of gauze and begins wiping down the wound as she glares at Wes. "This is the last time I see you," she tells him with a grimace.

"You already know that's not happening, July," my brother says as his jaw tics.

"No." She shakes her head, getting a new piece of gauze to clean the backside of my shoulder. "I know twice you've called me a bitch without cause." I wince at that, since my mom would skin me alive if she ever heard me call a woman a bitch. She shakes her head again then turns it so her gaze connects with his. "I know you made me feel like crap when you found my cousin in my house."

"I—" Wes starts, but she cuts him off.

"No, you didn't even ask; you just jumped to conclusions." She finishes cleaning my wound then looks at Wes again. "Then you show up at my house and ask me to do you a favor, refusing to tell me anything. So, yes, this is the last time we see each other. I think it's obvious we have no reason to stay in contact," she grumbles, and then frowns when she sees me smiling.

"You are so fucked, brother," I mumble, looking at Wes. He rolls his eyes at me as July starts to thread up the needle. It doesn't take long to get the wound closed up, and I don't even flinch as she works on me. Maybe it's the Jack, or maybe I'm in shock. Hell, it could be a little of both, but by the time she's finished putting a bandage over the stitched up wound, the sun is beginning to rise.

"Thanks, girly," I tell her, standing up from the kitchen table, and Wes shoos her off to bed while he and I clean up the mess.

On the drive back to our compound, Wes speaks up. "Correction: I think we're both fucked, bro."

"What do you mean?" I ask, quirking a brow at him.

"You've had a dreamy-ass look on your face ever since we left Kayan's place. You so much of a masochist that you're falling for a girl who shot you? We all know you like it rough, man, but goddamn." He chuckles.

I can't hide my smile. "My little kitten has claws," I say once more, leaning my head back against the headrest and thinking of the little woman who's filled my every thought since I met her.

3

KAYAN

It's been days since I shot Z. Freaking *days*. And I can't get that infuriating man out of my head.

Okay, so he's really not all that infuriating. But what he turns me into certainly is. I am not some timid little creature who needs to be watched over. I am definitely not the type of woman who allows a man to make her feel small and meek, no matter how tall and gorgeous he is... or how giant his biceps are.

I catch myself sighing dreamily at just... how... giant those damn biceps are, and shake myself out of it.

I'm not that kind of woman. Have never allowed myself to be that way, not even when I was young. I had to build up walls, grow thick skin, because my parents were, and still are, emotionless assholes. All they care about is their image.

On the outside, they are the perfect couple, with their perfect two-story house in the perfect neighborhood, with their perfect daughter, and their perfect freaking pets—a giant salt water tank of exotic fish that impresses anyone who comes over, which they pay someone else to tend to.

But on the inside, they are unforgiving, narcissistic hypocrites. It's a miracle I didn't turn out just like them. If it weren't for July and her family, I'm sure I would've. My parents allowed me to play with her at a very young age because they saw how genuinely "perfect" her parents were and they thought it'd boost their appearance by having their daughter associated with the town's beloved Mayson family. Uncle Asher and Aunt November weren't fooled, of course, but they didn't take it out on the kid— me. They welcomed me with open arms, because no matter how my parents were to their so-called friends, I was loyal to July.

One of the first times we played at her house and I got to hang out with her dog Beast, we decided right then and there we would be friends forever. I always joked it was because I always wanted an excuse to play with the huge Great Dane, but really it was the whole package. And when we got a little older and our noble pal passed away, it was then we made the pact to open up our own animal clinic. I was always super squeamish around blood though, so the actual doctoring part would be up to July. With my growing love of organization and natural technologic abilities, it would be up to me to take care of the business side of things. We were the perfect team. And still are.

Thinking of my aversion to blood, it dawns on me that I never even hesitated to help Z after I shot him. I put on the tourniquet and cleaned up his bloody arm without a moment's pause—well, except to throw him a little sass. My only thought had been to help the giant, beautiful man... even though he *had* just broken into my place.

Ugh! I need to get him out of my head. I've heard his motorcycle pass by my place a few times in the past couple days, but he hasn't actually approached me. It's just enough of a reminder of him that it pops him back into my damn mind.

Not that he ever left it.

No, I need a distraction. I need to go out.

Grabbing my phone off the side table next to my couch, I pull up Eric's messaging thread. He's an old flame I've known since high school. We're nothing serious; we decided a long, long time ago that we made much better friends than anything more. Every once in a while, when neither of us is in any type of relationship, we go grab dinner or catch a movie.

Me: **What's up, E? Doing anything tonight? I'm starving and bored.**

Eric: **Hey, darlin'. Where's your conjoined twin? Not attached at the hip tonight?**

Me: **Nah, she's with her hot new biker guy.**

The words immediately form images of another hot biker guy in my brain, and I shake away the thought.

Eric: **What you feel like eating?**

Me: **Hmmm... surprise me.**

Eric: **Okay, come snatch you up in 10.**

Me: Sounds good.

I DON'T PUT a lot of effort into getting ready. After all, it's just Eric. But I do pull my long, black hair down from its messy bun, brush it out, and put it back up in a slightly neater messy bun on top of my head. I trade out my fuzzy purple slippers for some Converse, and then plop down on my couch to wait for Eric.

I'm doing a little FBI work, going through Wes's friends list on Facebook to see if Z's image pops up—because obviously, "Z" wasn't exactly good for search results—when Eric sends me a text.

ERIC: **Here!**
Me: Coming down now.

I CLOSE out all my apps, shaking my head in disgust at myself for obsessing over a man whose real name I don't even know. I put LeFou in his crate and lock my door behind me, hurrying to Eric's car. When I slam the car door behind me, I poke him in his soft belly like I always do, making him chuckle.

"Ready to feed that cat dad bod?" I tease. It's what he calls it, now that he's turned into some kind of cat lady. Cat dude. Whatever. He basically keeps July and me in business he has so many beloved pets, and he'd much rather hang out at home with his furbabies than go to the gym. I mean, who wouldn't?

"Always." He grins, and he pulls out on the main road.

A while later, we pull into our favorite burger joint, and my stomach shows its immediate approval with a growl. After ordering our meals at the counter, we pick the booth we always end up sitting in and chat while we wait for our food.

"So what's been going on? I haven't seen you in a couple weeks," he prompts, taking a drink from his Dr. Pepper.

"Nothing really exci— wait. That's a lie. July and I went on a real stakeout the other night!" I whisper-hiss the last part.

"A... stakeout?" He laughs. "What, like, with sweet catsuits and snacks and stuff?"

"God, you know me way too well." I roll my eyes.

"Over a decade of friendship, Crazy One," he reminds me. He calls July "Crazy Two" when I'm telling him about our epic adventures. There have been quite a few over the years. She's my partner in crime.

"Fair enough. So. Someone has been leaving these poor injured... no, not even just injured. These dogs are basically taking their last breaths when this person leaves them at the door of our clinic for us to find the next morning," I confide quietly.

"Wait... like, it's happened more than once?" His eyes go wide.

"Several times now. It's obvious they're being fought, ya know, like for money. Anyway, so we had a stakeout and caught the dude dropping off a dog. We followed him, and—"

"Two American burgers all the way with fries?" We're interrupted by the waitress.

We lean back, realizing we were practically in each

other's face in the middle of the table as I told him the exciting but heartbreaking tale.

"That's us," Eric replies, rubbing his hands together.

I wiggle in my seat, a happy dance as I reach for the ketchup to soak my fries. Eric's chuckle makes me look up at him. "What?"

"I want a girl who reacts to me the way you react when someone brings you food," he tells me, and my face softens.

"Same, homie. Same." And that's when Z's face appears in my mind's eye for the first time in the last twenty minutes. But it's not just Z's face. It's the expression he wears whenever he looks at me. He looks at me like he wants to devour me, like I'm his prey. Probably exactly how I'm looking at this burger in front of me.

"So what happened after you followed him?" Eric asks a few minutes later, after we've inhaled half our meals without a single word between us.

I wipe my mouth with a napkin and swallow my bite of food with a sip of sweet tea. "We followed him to this biker bar. Super sketchy."

"In your catsuits, no less," he inserts with a chuckle.

"In our sweet-ass catsuits." I nod. "But our plan was thwarted!" I raise my fist in the air dramatically.

"Thwarted?" He raises a brow.

"Freaking. Thwarted." I sigh. "July's stupid hot biker was there and made us leave. So we never got to question the guy who's been dropping off the pups."

"Damn. Stupid hot bikers. They ruin everything," Eric says, shaking his head.

"Right?" I agree, thinking of Z and how he's ruined

my brain, making me unable to think of hardly anything but him.

We're so full by the time we're done eating that we decide going to see a movie would be a waste of money and would end up being an expensive nap. He takes me home instead, promising to send me pics of the new kitty obstacle course he's been building the last several weeks. I don't care what anyone says. I have the coolest friends ever.

I have a smile on my face as I unlock my door, my belly nice a full, and my Jacuzzi tub is calling my name. I can hear LeFou barking inside, so as I enter my house, I coo a "It's just me, little guy" as I close the door behind me.

As I reach for the switch on my couch-side lamp, I'm suddenly grabbed from behind. I don't even have time to scream before I'm slammed against the door, right next to the window Z came through nights ago. It knocks the breath out of me, and fear consumes me, knowing my gun is in the other room.

"WHAT HAPPENED?" July asks shakily, pulling me into the house after I somehow made it here in a daze and banged on her door.

I didn't know where else to go. My eyes fill up with tears and she helps me over to the couch, barely registering Wes is on his phone behind July.

"Talk to me," she urges, and I lower my head, trying to find the courage to relive the most terrifying experience of my life.

"Wait 'til Z and a couple of the guys get here," Wes interrupts, getting down on his haunches next to July and handing me some tissue.

"Why do we need to wait for them?" she asks him, looking into my watery eyes. I know I must have a black eye and a cut lip. It stings when my tears run across them.

"I only want her to tell us once, and then you're going to go clean her up," he explains gently.

She nods then moves to sit down next to me, wrapping her arm around my shoulders. I lean into her, her familiar presence comforting as we wait.

I don't know how much time passes, but the loud sound of motorcycle pipes pulls me out of my haze. I'm unsure how many guys are coming, but judging from the sound, it's way more than the couple Wes spoke of before.

"Be right back," he mutters, heading out the door and coming back a few minutes later with Z.

My heart skips a beat when my eyes land on him. And for some reason, all I want to do is run into his arms to let him protect me, to keep the monsters at bay. I don't even have it in me to scold myself for such weak thoughts.

"Fuck no," Z growls as soon as he sees me, and it makes me a little self-conscious, wondering just how bad I look right now.

I lift my hand to my hair, feeling to see what it must look like. Yep, just as I thought. Hot mess express. His jaw starts ticking, and his arms, which were at his sides, lift to cross over his chest like he's trying to control himself. I wish I had the courage to tell him not to. I wish he'd rush over to me, pick me up, and cradle me to that wide, muscular chest, those hulking arms enfolding me and never letting me go.

"Are you going to be okay talking in front of them?" July asks me, and I nod, taking her hand in mine to keep from doing something stupid like beg Z to hold me.

"I went out with Eric to get some food," I start, and a growl fills the room.

July's head flies up to look at Z with a glare. "Can you control yourself?" she snaps, and he lifts his chin. The compulsion to go to him is even stronger, wanting to assure him that Eric is just a friend and he has nothing to worry about. But that's just silly. Z and I are nothing to each other. Why should I feel like I need to assure him about another man?

"So you went out with Eric, and then what happened?" July prompts.

"Um." I shake my head and pull my eyes from Z to look at her, trying to focus on telling them what happened instead of the man across the room that seems to take up all the air in the whole house. "He dropped me home and when I got inside my apartment, I was shoved into the door and someone grabbed me around the throat. They told me I needed to give you a warning."

"What?" July whispers, squeezing my hand tighter as fear fills her every feature.

"They said if we don't stop sticking our noses where they don't belong, we will find out what happens to nosey little girls." I gulp, and watch her look at Wes, whose gaze travels from Z's to hers.

"What did they look like?" Z questions, and his deep voice coats my chest in both calmness and excitement, making me jittery.

"All I saw was a tattoo of a spider on his forehead. Really, I was too scared to pay much attention," I reply, and more tears fill my eyes.

"It's going to be okay," July tries to assure me, and both of us look toward the front door as Z leaves, slamming the door behind him and making me jump. I immediately feel his absence, and my body slumps into the couch as if he took every bit of my energy with him.

"Baby," Wes calls. "Go get her cleaned up. I'm heading out with the boys. Harlen and Everret will be outside."

"Okay," she agrees, and I'm vaguely aware of it as he bends over and kisses her before he's gone too.

I try to shake myself out of the fog I'm in, resorting to my first and foremost defense mechanism—humor.

"So I'm guessing I don't need a new calendar?" I ask her, referring to the one Wes wrote all over at work, marking July busy for lunch every single day for the foreseeable future. At the time, she was pissed, but now, she can't even try to hide the smile lighting her eyes. "What a difference a few days makes." I laugh.

"You're hilarious." She rolls her eyes. "Now, let's get you cleaned up before Z comes back," she says, and my teasing grin immediately turns into a wide-eyed look of panic.

"You know I can't deal with scary hot," I whisper, and my vision goes cloudy.

"So you've said." She takes my hand and leads me toward her bedroom, where she helps me get cleaned up.

4

Z

We've spent the last couple hours finding out everything we can about the person with the spider tattoo who broke into Kayan's apartment and put their hands on her. When I left July's house, I was ready to find the fucker and rip his head from his fucking spine. Unfortunately, we didn't find out much, and we ended up talking with July's cousin Jax.

Back at July's house, I stand back by the door while Wes talks to his woman, and I see the moment Kayan comes awake on the couch next to them.

"I talked to Jax," Wes is saying to July. "Between his boys and mine, we'll be able to figure this out." He pulls July closer to him with a hand behind her neck. "I'm going to stay here with you and your friend until we can get some security in at her place and yours."

"Uh, what—?" she whispers.

"That's not happening," Kayan cuts in, making her consciousness known. "Whoever did this isn't going to scare me out of my own home. I love you, but I'm not staying here."

This doesn't surprise me one bit. She told me the night she shot me at her place that she liked her space and refused to move in with July.

"It's not safe for you to be there alone," July says softly, but Kayan stands up, crossing her arms over her chest.

"They are not scaring me out of my house," she repeats.

"You're not staying alone," I finally speak up, stepping into the room more.

"You're not my dad," she replies, and her sassiness makes my dick twitch.

"You're not staying alone, kitten," I repeat, leaning forward and getting into her space.

"Fine, I'll call Eric." She shrugs, and I can see she's purposely trying to bait me, obviously remembering my reaction earlier when she said she went out to dinner with him. It works.

"Think again," I tell her, narrowing my eyes.

"You can't tell me what to do!" she shouts, stomping her foot.

"Bet your sweet ass I can!" I holler back, and Wes's dog Capone starts to bark at us.

"I'm going home!" she cries, throwing her hands up in the air in frustration while I glare at her.

"Okay, then I'm staying with you," I say, sweeping my hand toward the door.

"What?" Kayan stops, her body freezing almost comically.

"I'm staying with you," I repeat.

"Uhh..." She looks at July like she just realized what she had gotten herself into, and her friend smiles. "Maybe I'll just stay here," Kayan whispers.

"Nope," I snap, shaking my head. "Walk your sweet ass to your car. I'll follow you home."

"Um..." She glances at July once more, and I can tell by the way she presses her lips together that July's trying to keep from laughing. "Fine." She glares at me then looks at the other woman. "I'm quitting tomorrow."

"You were already fired," July tells her, and my brow furrows until I realize it must be an inside joke.

"I hate you," she grumbles at me as she stomps toward the door, but all I can do is watch her sexy ass as she passes by and heads out the front door.

"Please be nice to her," July pleas, stealing my attention, and I give her a look, lift my chin, and then leave, shutting the door behind me.

5

KAYAN

"**W**hat the hell have you gotten yourself into, woman?" I ask myself, turning into my driveway and watching in my rearview mirror as Z pulls in behind me on his motorcycle.

It's true—some of my normal attitude had shown itself when I'd first woken up in July's living room, and in my fog, I'd forgotten for a split second just who I was dealing with. But the moment that man got in my face and said he'd be staying with me, my mind was bombarded with images of his big body filling up my space. Which led to thoughts of his big body filling *me* up.

I flash back to the night I met him, when he and Wes caught us at Momma's Country after we followed the guy who was leaving the dogs at the clinic.

"WHAT?" *I mumble as July wakes me up, where I'm in the car* seat next to her. I wipe the doughnut frosting from my face. Half the fun of a stakeout is the snacks, after all.

"They're here," she hisses, and my head comes up, my eyes wide.

"Oh shit," I whisper, pulling the camera off the dash.

July pulls out her phone and calls Mark, one of the vets who's been working at our clinic over the last few months. She tells him he needs to get to the office and take care of the dog that was just dropped off, and to call the vet tech on call. We watch as the person drops the dog at the door of our clinic then gets back in their truck.

I can tell July wants to go to the poor animal, but knowing there will be someone coming to help him soon keeps her in place and focused on our task at hand. We need information, so we can do what we can to stop this from happening any longer. When the person pulls out, July keeps her headlights off before starting up the Jeep and following him out of the parking lot.

"I wonder where he's going," she says aloud as we head out of town on one of the back roads.

"Don't know," I mumble, watching the truck in the distance, which pulls into a large parking lot packed with cars. It's a Friday night, and this place is hoppin'.

July pulls in and parks a few spaces behind him then waits until the driver gets out before she opens the door of her Jeep, and I hurry to meet her at the back of the vehicle.

"Just so you know, I'm firing you on Monday," she tells me, gesturing to our matching outfits I made her wear.

"You look smoking hot," I whisper, but I'm totally as nervous as she clearly is.

With a shake of her head, we head into the building. The moment we walk through the door, my ears are assaulted by *the twangy sound of country music, making me grimace. We follow the guy toward the bar, feeling every single person's eyes in the place locked on July and me. Shit, if I were them, I'd totally be staring too. How often do you see two chicks dressed like cat-women walk into a country western bar?*

"Your dad's in back, bud," the bartender tells the guy we followed from the clinic. He looks younger than us, maybe twenty-one, especially when he takes his hat off. He runs his hand over his hair then gets up from the stool he just occupied and starts walking toward the back of the bar.

We're headed in that direction, when someone wraps their arm around July, and I barely hear him say, "Where you going, pretty girl?" over the loud music. My girl elbows the guy, making me proud, and she grabs my hand, pulling me in the direction the guy had now disappeared.

"You're really getting fired," she tells me, and I can't help but grin before I run into her back where she's halted in place. When I look up at her then follow her line of vision, I see who she's spotted, and he definitely does not look happy to see us.

"Oh no," I whisper, watching as Wes puts down his pool stick.

"Run," July hisses.

"What?" My brow furrows as I look at her.

"I said run!" she cries, and we both turn and start toward the front of the bar. We get down the hall, when July's hand is suddenly jerked out of mine.

"What the fuck are you wearing?" I hear Wes growl, and I know I'm totally fired.

"What are you doing here?" July asks, struggling in his hold.

"Z, watch her," Wes says, and I see he's talking to someone behind me. I turn around and stop in my tracks, eye-level with

a ridiculously wide chest covered in a white tank and leather vest. My lips part as my eyes travel up... up... and up impossibly higher. And that's when they land on the most terrifyingly gorgeous man I've ever seen in my twenty-six years on this earth.

He's so freaking tall, with a shaved head, short beard, and tattoos that run from his thick neck, and down his arms that would give Thor a run for his money. His muscles look even more intimidating as he crosses his arms over his chest, looking down at me and my 5'2" frame. He's more than a foot taller than me, but he makes me feel even smaller the way his eyes devour me in my catsuit. Dark chocolate eyes, almost black. Mine narrow, trying to place what his heritage might be. Hispanic? Maybe Persian? I can't tell exactly, but he's rocking a tan I'm completely jealous of.

"That's not necessary. We were just leaving," July inserts, but when I glance behind me, I see her disappear into the men's restroom as Wes forces her inside.

When I look back up at the hulking man in front of me, I try to come up with something witty to say in order to get myself out of here faster, so I can just wait outside in July's Jeep for her, but nothing comes out but a nervous giggle.

"What's your name, little one?" His voice is so deep it vibrates straight down my spine and makes my knees practically knock together.

"K-Kayan," I squeak out, and clear my throat, taking a step backward. Maybe putting some space between me and him will help me ditch this timid thing I've suddenly become.

"Kayan," he purrs, as if tasting my name on his tongue. He smiles, and his teeth are startlingly white in his tan face. He takes a step forward as I take another one back, until I find myself between him and the wall next to the restroom. I find it *hard to meet his eyes he's so blatantly beautiful, so I stare at my shoes. He doesn't say anything else, but seems to stand guard over me, blocking me from everyone's view.*

Moments later, Wes exits the men's room, pulling July behind him, who looks suspiciously flushed.

"I remember you," she tells Z, and my eyes dart between them. I'll have to ask her later where she met him before.

"Let's get the girls out of here, and then we'll come back and finish up," Wes states.

"Sure," Z mutters, and he wraps a hand around my waist as I struggle out of his grasp.

Out in the parking lot, I'm hyperaware of his closeness. I can feel his eyes on me, and it's both exhilarating and unnerving.

"You're as shy as a kitten. Don't think I've ever had shy in my bed," Z growls, not bothering to lower his volume in front of our friends, and I feel my face flame viciously. I can't even come up with a sassy retort as I take my place in the passenger seat of July's Jeep. All I can do is stare into my lap, too shaken to my core to meet his gaze I feel burning into me. "Be good, kitten," he rumbles, shutting my door.

"Straight home," I hear Wes tell July.

"Straight home," she repeats.

"We have some shit to work out, but I'll get in there," he tells her, before adding, "Be good."

She nods and he slams her door. She starts up the Jeep and pulls out of the lot then looks over at me at a stop sign. When my eyes meet hers, I swallow hard then feel my face split into a grin.

"That was scary, but oh... my... God," I breathe, making her giggle.

"No more stakeouts," she tells me.

I snort and whisper, "No more stakeouts."

A knock at my window makes me jump, pulling me from the memory. I look to my left and see his half-worried, handsome face.

"You gonna sleep in your car, kitten?" Z asks, and when I shake my head dumbly, he opens the door, holding his hand out to me.

The flashback was a reminder of how overwhelming his presence is. My feistiness from earlier leaves me, especially as we walk up to my front door and the memory of being grabbed inside my house overtakes all thoughts. I whimper on the first porch step, spinning around to run back to my car, but my face plants right into Z's neck.

His arms immediately come around me, wrapping me up in a warm, safe, delicious-smelling cocoon.

"I'm here now, little one. Ain't nothin' bad going to happen while I'm with you. I can promise you that," he murmurs at the side of my head, and I can't help but relax in his embrace.

It's like I've finally come home, which is funny, since we're standing in front of my actual house that felt like anything but home only seconds before. "He.... I... I didn't even see him coming, Z. He was already inside when I got here, and he grabbed me from behind." I turn my face further into his skin and rest my head where his shoulder is still bandaged where I shot him.

"I know, baby. I doubt he came back tonight, but I'm going to go in first and check everything out, okay?"

I realize my fingers are gripping his leather vest when I feel my nails dig in deeper before letting go with a nod.

With one last deep inhale of his intoxicating scent, I lift my head out of its nook and step to the side, allowing him to pass me up the stairs to my front door. I hand him my keys and watch him unlock the door before he steps inside.

My hands twist together as I wait for him on my porch, every sound making me jittery as I wait for either a fight to ring out into the late night air or for someone to come running out my front door in order to escape Z's wrath. Because I have no doubt, from the look in his eyes when I was telling everyone what happened earlier, and from the conviction in his voice when he just promised me nothing would happen while he's with me, Z would tear the intruder limb from limb with his capable bare hands.

6

Z

"All clear, kitten," I tell her, reaching out the front door with my hand outstretched to where she huddles by the porch steps. She takes a look at my open palm as if it's a snake that might bite her, but then relaxes and puts her tiny hand in mine. Pulling her into her living room, it's then I realize her dog never once barked at me while I was checking around her house.

She must notice too, because she immediately bends at the waist to check inside his crate. "Bonjour, LeFou. How's my baby?"

The little dog immediately unburies himself from all his blankets, giving a rough shake before trembling with excitement. She unlatches the door and picks him up, allowing him to lick beneath her chin as she giggles. Glancing up at me, she must see the strange look on my face, because she asks, "What?"

"You just greeted your Chihuahua in French." I raise a brow.

"So?" She pops a hip, trying to look sassy as she holds

the little creature, its bug eyes seeming to bulge even more as his licking gets more aggressive.

"A Chihuahua who you named LeFou," I point out.

"Yeaaah?" she drawls.

"Aren't Chihuahuas supposed to be Mexican?" I prompt.

She gives a shrug, making a move for the sliding glass back door so she can let him out to do his business. "Maybe, but LeFou was like... one of the most loyal sidekicks in the history of ever. In his eyes, Gaston could do no wrong. And I needed a little companion who thought of me that way."

"Didn't LeFou end up switching sides at the very end of the movie?" I knew this would draw a smile out of her.

"I didn't take you for a Disney guru, Z. I'm impressed," she says with a grin. "And yes, you're right. But Gaston totally deserved it. I'd like to think I'd never be so villainous that *my* LeFou would ever need to turn on me."

I chuckle, shaking my head as I slip my cut off my shoulders and hang it on the back of one of her dining chairs. "Fair enough," I concede, watching her eyes heat as I then pull my black tank top over my head.

"W-what are you doing?" she stammers, her gaze roaming all over my naked chest.

"Getting ready for bed, kitten. It's pretty late, so I was going to crash on your couch. No one would be able to get past me if they tried to come in the window or door," I explain.

LeFou scratches on the glass door, making her jump a little. She slides it open, and he prances in, going straight for his food dish.

"Oh. Yeah. That makes sense." She pours a small cupful of kibble into his dish then fills the water bowl up, scratching behind his ear before standing once more. "Let me grab you a pillow and a blanket really quick."

At my nod, she disappears down her hall for a moment before returning with a pillow and a floral throw blanket. When I take them from her, her scent fills my nostrils. They must be off her bed. I toss them on the couch and then take a seat next to them, sliding my black boots off then my socks. Without a word, she pulls out a dining chair at the kitchen table a couple feet away and takes a seat facing me.

"You all right?" I ask her, because she's just sitting there watching me, not saying anything.

She seems to shake herself. "Y-yeah. I just.... You're just making yourself right at home, getting naked in my living room. Like it's no big deal."

The corner of my lips pulls up. "Not naked. Just more comfortable. And it's not a big deal. I'm hear to keep you safe, to give you peace of mind so you can get a good night's sleep."

Her face goes soft, and relief fills me. Could this mean she's finally going to stop fighting this feeling between us?

Her voice gentles. "It's a big deal to me."

"Why's that, kitten?" I lean back into the couch cushions.

"Well... I've never had a half-naked guy in my house before. Plus, I've never had a guy who insisted on being my personal bodyguard. This is all a little... overwhelming," she confesses. "*You're* a little overwhelming." She pulls her bottom lip between her teeth.

I make it to her in one long stride, and she gasps, glancing between me and the couch, as if she's trying to figure out how I got to her so quickly from where I'd been sitting. My arm circles around her lower back and I effortlessly pull her out of her seat and against my bare chest. And before she can even make a sound of disagreement, my mouth is on hers. I don't know what possessed me to claim her in this moment, but her admission of never having brought a guy back to her place before flipped a switch inside me. Virgin territory. My body screams for me to christen the place, to make love to Kayan and be the first to mark her space as mine.

She whimpers into my mouth as I slide my tongue between her soft lips. I'm as gentle as possible, since I don't want to make the cut on her lip hurt worse, and I feel her relax in my embrace, allowing me to take all her weight. My hand slides up between her shoulder blades then into her hair, my big hand engulfing the back of her skull, making it easy to manipulate her position. I kiss her deep, until my soul pours down her throat and dances with hers. Her fingers dig into my biceps, holding on for dear life as she fully gives herself over to me.

My grip falls to her ass and I lift her up, her legs wrapping around my hips, and I feel her ankles lock behind me. Without breaking our kiss, I make my way to her bedroom, sprawling us across her comforter as my weight presses her into the mattress. She moans as she grinds her hips against me, moving like a cat in heat.

"That's it, kitten," I growl against her lips. "Show me how bad you want me."

She shudders, shaking her head slightly, but not

enough to disengage our mouths. "What are you doing to me, Z?" she whispers.

I nip her bottom lip, tilting my hips to give her better friction as she continues to move. I feel her heat through our jeans as if she's naked. I can only imagine how wet she is.

"Z." She takes a breath. "Z? My God, I don't even know your real name, and I want you more than I've ever wanted anyone in my life. How is that even possible?"

I pull back to look down into her beautiful eyes, a small smile on my face. "It's Eleazar. Zar for short, and then it got shortened even more to just Z."

Her hips thrust upward and she groans. "Oh, God. That was so hot. Say it again, just like you did before."

I chuckle, having never repeated my own name over and over in bed before. But I do it, just to make her happy. "Eleazar," I say, rolling the R, my Hispanic heritage on full display in the proper pronunciation.

"So you're what? Mexican? Puerto Rican? I know nothing about you, and all I want is for you to be inside me. This is so... wrong," she murmurs.

I swallow, holding onto my self-control at her admission. I'd rather take it slow and answer her questions than to rush through our first time and have her regret it. "Spaniard. My parents are first generation Americans, and their parents were from a small town outside Madrid."

She nods. "Oh, that's nice." She circles her hips, her eyes nearly crossing at the friction. "I'd love to visit somewhere exotic like that some day. I've never left the country before."

Her rambling reminds me of the first time I met her,

when I told her I'd never had shy in my bed before. So I talk to her, putting her at ease as I begin to undress her. "I'll take you there some day, kitten. I'll take you anywhere you wanna go. Just name it." I slide her top off, tossing it to the floor before reaching for the button on her jeans. "I was in the Navy. Joined because I had dreams of seeing the world. I went to many places. But there's so many more I'd like to see. And I'd love to see them with you. Even the ports I've been before. I could take you and show you all the best hidden spots. Your own personal tour guide."

She smiles, closing her eyes as I pull her jeans down her shapely legs. "My own personal bodyguard, and now my own personal tour guide? I'm never getting rid of you, am I?"

"Never. Once I make you mine, there's no turning back, little one. You'll be stuck with me forever," I tell her, kissing a trail up the inside of her thigh until I reach her panty-covered center. She pants as I hook my thumb in the elastic and remove them from her body in one swift jerk, baring her to me. I glance up at her face, seeing she still has her eyes locked closed, but she's not trying to stop me, so I continue my perusal.

I breathe in her scent, the aroma making my already hard cock throb behind my zipper painfully, so I reach down, unbutton and unzip my jeans, and pull them off swiftly, leaving me fully naked. The first swipe of my tongue up her slit makes her jerk as if she's been electro-cuted, so I thread my arms around her legs, the backs of her thighs resting against my shoulders as my hands grip, spreading her pussy open so I can get to the sweet spot.

"Holy fu—!" she cries, as I suck her sensitive flesh

into my hot mouth, her back arching, her head pressing into the bed as I lock her lower half in place. There's no way she's getting away from me now, not when I've finally gotten my first taste of her.

Fucking heaven.

"Anything else you wanna know, kitten?" I growl against her clit.

She lets out a long moan as I flick the tip of my tongue along her folds. "No! No more questions. Just. Don't. Freaking. Stop!"

I grin to myself before giving her pussy my full attention, eating her relentlessly until she's writhing and panting incoherent appreciation. And soon, her muscles seize before she calls out my name, my real name, and her juices spill onto my tongue as she comes. It takes everything in me not to come right then and there, my cock pressing into her mattress as she melts, her entire body going lax.

I kiss the inside of her thigh, discreetly wiping my face there. I don't know how she'd feel about me kissing her with so much of her wetness covering my jaw, so instead of finding out this first time we're together, I'll save that discovery for later. As I crawl up her body, I can't help but notice how tiny she is beneath me, how small she is compared to my 6'5" frame. It makes me feel powerful in this moment, even though I know my heart is helpless against her.

I nudge her opening with my cock, and the heat and wetness of her brings me back from the brink for a second. "I don't have a condom, kitten." Hopefully she has one nearby or I might die if I can't sink inside her tightness.

"I... I don't either." She bites her lip, finally opening her eyes and looking up at me. "But I'm on birth control. Are you...?"

I know she's asking if I'm clean. I am. But I've never been inside a woman without a glove before. The thought seems foreign. Almost taboo.

But as I look down into her beautiful eyes, the need I see there calls to me. And as I told her before, once I have her, she's mine forever. I wasn't fucking around. Something inside me just knows she's the one. The one I'm meant to spend my life with.

"I'm clean. But just so you know, I've never done this before," I confess, and her eyebrows lift in surprise.

"You're... you're a virgin?" she practically gasps.

I nearly collapse on top of her I laugh so hard, my cock bouncing against her slick entrance, sobering me quickly. "No, kitten. I've just never done it without a condom before. So I don't know how this is gonna go. You could turn me into a two-pump chump."

Her face softens, and she reaches up to cup my jaw. "Trust me, Z. It's not gonna take much for me. You've already made me feel things I've never felt be— Ohhhh-hh," she groans as I sink into her, my arms nearly buckling at how glorious her pussy feels gripping me.

I feel her legs come up and lock around my ass, and her muscles squeeze, urging me to start moving. And move, I do.

I start off slow, gliding in and out with calculated strokes, feeling my throbbing cock disappear into her depths. And at her little mewls and sighs, my control snaps, and my pace picks up until her headboard is pounding against the wall and her voice gives out from crying out with every plunge.

It's the sexiest thing I've ever heard, Kayan coming undone beneath me. She grips my biceps, turning her head and sinking her teeth into my flesh as her pussy spasms around me and she comes. The slight pain my kitten's little fangs induces is all it takes, and I explode inside her, a bark of passion and relief echoing around her room as the most intense orgasm of my entire life overtakes my entire being.

She whimpers in protest as I carefully slide out of her, but then her eyes widen as they meet mine once again. "Oh my God, I bit you. What the hell is wrong with me? I'm so so—"

"Baby. It was the hottest thing ever. I know we have a lot to learn about one another, but just know, for future reference, there's nothing I love more with my pleasure than a little pain," I tell her, giving her just a hint of the type of sex I enjoy most. I don't want to freak her out, but she needs to know the truth about me if I'm going to have the privilege of keeping her and making her mine forever.

"Oh. Well then. I uh... I'm glad you liked it." She blushes, and I climb off the bed to go into the bathroom.

"Where're your washcloths, kitten?" I ask, reaching for the cabinet beneath the sink.

"Second drawer on the left," she replies, and I open it instead, snatching up a gray washcloth and turning on the faucet to let the water warm up.

Wringing out the rag, I walk back over to where she's still sprawled on top of her comforter. I press it gently to her core and hear her sigh as it soothes the ache there.

She was so tight, and I'm not small by any means, my cock proportional to the rest of my large frame.

When she's all cleaned up, I toss the cloth into the sink to take care of later. Right now, all I want to do is wrap around the tiny woman in her bed and fall asleep with her in my arms.

7

KAYAN

It's only two hours later when the alarm on my phone goes off, letting me know it's time to get up and ready for work. I glare at it, where it sits on my kitchen table, wishing it would understand if I cussed it out and told it I was up already, since I never went back to sleep last night.

After Z fell asleep, my white sheet twisted around his naked lower half, contrasting dramatically with his beautiful tan and tattooed skin, I couldn't fall asleep myself.

What the hell had I just done? I barely knew the man, and I had slept with him? Sure, there was an undeniable connection between us. I was pulled toward him with the force of the strongest magnet in the world. And it sounded like if he had it his way, we would be a "thing."

I hadn't been a "thing" with anyone in a very long time. I've only slept with men I was in a serious relationship with, which, before last night, was a grand total of two.

"God, this is so freaking backward," I groan into my half-empty coffee mug. Isn't it usually the woman who wants a relationship, and the man who fights her off as long as he can?

Well... no, actually. If Wes and July are anything to go by.

"What is with these bossy-ass bikers?" I mumble to myself. "They think they can just roll up on their sexy motorcycles, in their sexy leather cuts, and be like, 'You, woman. Mine!' and we'll be all swoony and shit and just agree."

"Yes. That's exactly what we think," Z's amused voice comes from behind me, making me jump and slosh a little coffee onto my hand and table. I glare over my shoulder and watch through slitted eyes as he approaches, trying my best to ignore the deep V at his hips, where his jeans are slung low.

Before I know what he's doing, he pulls my wet hand to his lips and sucks the coffee off my fingers, causing my core to clench. It makes me undeniably aware of the soreness there, and my cheeks flush.

"Mmm, mind if I have a cup of that?" he asks low.

"S-sure. The K-cups are in the drawer under the Keurig," I reply, hating the way he can zap all my sassiness with one lick of his skillful tongue.

"I wasn't talking about the coffee—" He glances down at my lap, as if he can smell my arousal there. "—but I guess that'll have to do, since I know you have to get to work soon."

My stomach twists with a surge of need, and I stand abruptly. "Uh. Right. Yeah. I gotta go get ready. Help yourself to whatever you want... in the kitchen. The food, I mean. Yeah." I shake my head and pull my hand from him, ignoring his chuckle as I hurry to my master bathroom.

I take the fastest shower in history, because I have no doubt if I'm in here longer than what it takes to soap up and rinse off, I'll have an unwanted—or so I tell myself—visitor, thanks to my bathroom door not having a lock. The damn room has a pocket door, which I never worried about before, living alone with no one to walk in on me.

I throw on my scrubs for the day, white ones covered in every Disney dog character. Even though I'm not a vet tech or anything, I choose to dress like July at work, to give us a uniformed and professional look, but mostly because it's like wearing comfy pajamas all day. I tie up my non-slip tennis shoes and grab my purse, heading into the living room.

Z is fully dressed, lounging on my couch and typing something into his phone. When he looks up and spots me, his face softens and he stands. "Ready to go?" he asks, pulling his key out of his pocket.

"Uh... yeah. But I don't need you to follow me. I'm just going straight to work from here," I tell him, pulling my own keys out of my purse.

He doesn't respond, just gives me a look that says he's going to do what he wants whether I like it or not. I roll my eyes and pass him on my way out the door.

Every glance in my rearview mirror makes my blood boil. How dare he look so freaking hot, cruising on his dark green Harley, seeming like he doesn't have a care in the world? Images of those outstretched, tattooed arms flash through my mind, but instead of gripping handle-bars like they are now, I remember the way they bulged and rippled as he braced himself above me last night, holding his weight up as he slid inside me.

By the time I park in front of the clinic, I'm an irri-tated mess, and I hop out of my car, slamming the door and throwing my purse on my shoulder.

"I told you I didn't need you to follow me!" I yell over my shoulder at Z, who sits on his bike with his arms crossed over his chest, watching my every move with a smirk on his irresistible face.

"Have a good day, kitten," is all he says, and I shake my head then storm over to July, stomping as I cross the parking lot. When I reach her side, I grab her arm and pull her toward the door of the building.

"Can I close the door to my car and get my coffee?" she asks, biting her lip, obviously trying to control her laughter.

I let go of her. "This isn't funny." I pout. "This is all your fault. Thanks to you, I had to have that guy in my house last night and this morning."

"I could think of much worse problems, honey," she tells me, slamming her door with her hip and grabbing her to-go coffee cup off the roof of her car.

I still can't believe I slept with him. It's such an un-Kayan thing to do. So much so, I don't even know how to tell July. So I decide to keep it to myself until I sort out my feelings about the whole situation.

"You *would* think so." I need to vent just a little, so I tell her, without giving everything away, "He was shirt-less in my house. Who gets undressed in front of people they don't know then struts around showing off their body?" I feel a little guilty, omitting what happened after Z became shirtless last night. Not to mention, he saw me naked first, when I shot him. I blow a piece of hair out of my face, which has turned hot at the memory.

"You like him." She gives me a smile then laughs at me.

"I do not like him." I frown, and we both watch as he pulls out of the parking lot, me having to control the dreamy sigh that wants to escape at how freaking gorgeous that damn man is.

"Sure, you don't," July says, seeing right through me.

"I don't," I retort, stomping past her as soon as she unlocks the door. "And if he thinks he's staying at my house tonight, he has another think coming!" I yell to her as she disappears into her office.

A few hours later, the front door chimes, and I unconsciously scoot my rolling chair back several feet at the infuriated look on the man's face. He looks familiar, and I squint my eyes, trying to place him. Then it hits me. Even though we were always a safe distance behind him the night we followed him to the biker bar, this is undeniably the guy who's been dropping off the fighting dogs.

"You," I squeak then clear my throat. "You're the guy—"

"Whatever you planned on doing the other night when you followed me, you need to forget it. You have no idea who you're dealing with," he growls, his deep voice not matching his young looks.

Before I can respond, July walks up to my desk, sweeping her eyes over me to see if I'm okay. "Can I help you?" she asks when she looks over at the guy.

"Like I was just telling your friend, you guys need to mind your business."

"I need to mind my business?" She steps toward him and to my surprise pokes a finger in his chest. "You made whatever it is you're doing *my business* when you started dropping dead dogs off at my hospital."

I nod, scooting my chair forward and silently giving my best friend support. I tamp down my urge to stand up and say, "Yeah!"

"I was trying to do the right thing, but I won't be able to save your stupid asses again. They will kill you," he says, and I suck in a breath at his rudeness.

But July takes a much different approach than I would have, if I were taking over this situation. "I know people who can help you," she tells him gently, and it makes me look at him more closely. He's definitely as young as we originally thought, around twenty years old. But his blue eyes look exhausted, as if he's seen much more in his years than he should have. He seems to take in July's words, as if wishing he could get the assistance she's offering. "They can help; I promise," she adds, and he shakes himself, his eyes turning angry.

"Just mind your fucking business!" he shouts then turns around and pushes so hard against the door that the glass cracks as it hits the outside of the building.

"I wonder what we're missing," July says aloud as we both watch him screech out of the parking lot.

"I don't know, but he seems scared," I reply, thinking about the flash of longing I saw in his face.

"Yeah," she agrees, swallowing.

"Do you want me to call Wes or Z and tell them what

just happened?" I ask, and she meets my gaze and shakes her head.

"No, if anything else happens, I'll tell him," she promises.

I pooch my lips out doubtfully, but I nod anyway.

8

Z

"Um. Hello. Excuse me. What the hell are you doing in my house... again?" Kayan's sweet, haughty voice is thrown at me from her front door.

I slide my arm up across the back of her couch and watch her eyes heat when they land on it. I haven't figured out if it's the muscles or the tattoos that make her practically forget her name. Maybe it's both. In any case, I'll continue working out the rest of my life just to keep getting that look from her.

"Told you already, kitten. Ain't never letting you go." I watch her roll her eyes, and then ask, "How was your day today?"

"Yeah, you said that in like... the throes of passion. Guys don't mean stuff when they're balls-deep in some chick—"

"As good as your sweet pussy was, Kayan—" My use of her real name makes her head jerk back. Good, she's paying attention. "—not even it is good enough to make me lie to you. Nothing is. And I meant every single word I said while we were making love."

"Making lo— Ugh. You're annoying."

She crosses her arms over her scrub top-covered chest and plops down on the couch as far away from me as possible, which is laughable, because it's barely bigger than a loveseat. But I can tell by the look in her eyes she's putting on a front. My words hit home. She's just trying to save face. But why?

I try again to move along the conversation. "How was your day, kitten?

She visibly deflates, rolling in on herself and putting her head in her hands, her elbows resting on her knees. I want to pick her up and pull her onto my lap, rock her until everything is all better in her mind. But I stay where I am, hoping she'll open up to me.

"Don't tell Wes, but that guy showed up at the clinic today," she murmurs, and my brow furrows.

"The guy? The one with the spider tattoo?" I growl, pissed she hadn't called me as soon as it happened.

She waves her hand at me, shaking her head. "No, no... you freaking bear. Calm your tits. The guy July and I followed, the young one who's been dropping the injured dogs off at the clinic."

"That's barely any better. They're all connected some-how, and next time, your ass better tell me as soon as possible," I order, and her narrowed eyes turn to me.

"Excuse you. You can't just order me about! We didn't know the other even existed a week ago, and suddenly you think you can tell me 'my ass better' do something? You've got a lot to learn." She stands from the couch and stomps to her room, slamming her door.

All I can do is smirk and adjust my rock-hard cock behind my zipper. I fucking love it when her feistiness comes out to play. Almost as much as I like her shy. But she's the one who has a lot to learn. I'm not backing down. She's mine. All fucking mine. And in being mine, she's going to have to start turning to me for help instead of fighting me every step of the way. She's obviously been on her own for a long time, the epitome of an independent woman. I know it'll take some reconditioning to get her to actually lean on me, but I'm willing to put in the work. Nothing she does or says will push me away.

A few minutes later, after I've called Wes to let him know the girls received a visitor at work today, she storms out of her room, now dressed in skinny jeans that fit her like a second skin and a loose-fitting tee. "You did *not* just call Wes and tell him, after I specifically told you not to!" she yells, obviously having heard me through the door. She glares at me as she snatches up her purse, and then turns to stomp toward the front door, stopping to dig her key out of it.

"Where we going?" I ask right behind her, making her squeal as she spins around to look up at me.

She puts her hand to my chest and shoves, moving herself backward instead of me, and I fight my grin. "*We*... are going nowhere. *I*... am hungry, because I skipped lunch when the dog fighter guy came and gave me anxiety. But now I'm angry, not anxious. Which means I'm hangry. And you do not want to see me hangry," she threatens, and all I want to do is pet her hair and tell her how fucking adorable she is.

"I'm coming with you," I say matter-of-factly. "What do you want to eat?" I try to pull her key out of her hand, but she snatches her arm back, hitting her elbow against the door and wincing.

"Mother*trucker*, that freaking hurt! Gah! Go away!" She spins to pull open the door, but I wrap my arm around her waist, pulling her back against my front, and rub her elbow with my other hand, soothing away the ache. I feel her instantly melt against me.

"I'm going to feed my little kitten. You're not going anywhere alone, not after someone broke into your house just last night. You're going to have to get over it. You have people who care about you, and it's okay to allow them to protect you," I murmur into the side of her head, and she twitches in my arms, obviously trying to hold strong in her frustrating beliefs. But when she speaks, her voice is much calmer.

"Fine. But I don't want restaurant food. I want bestie food. Plus, I need to check on her, since you're a big freakin' tattletale. We're going to July's," she tells me, and I nod reluctantly. I was hoping to take her out to eat just the two of us, to try to get to know each other a little better. But if she needs the buffer of her best friend for now, then I'll allow it, because at least she's saying "we" instead of just her.

When we arrive at July's, I see Wes's bike parked in the driveway and pull in next to it. I had to practically wrestle the keys from Kayan before we left, but there was no way I was letting her drive me around like some pussy. It put her right back into her sassy-ass mood.

She jumps out of the car before I even put the gear in Park, making me growl and jump out after her, stalking her to the front porch. She tries to barge in, but is stopped abruptly by the locked door, so she lifts her fist and pounds with all the strength in her tiny body.

"July, open the door right now!" she yells, tapping her foot.

"Kitten," I rumble next to her, wishing she'd calm down just a little. Knowing she hasn't eaten today, I don't want her to pass out if she gets too upset.

She pounds on the door again, more frantically this time, and I do the only thing I can think of to snap her out of it. I grab her upraised hand from the wooden door and spin her toward me, my other hand going into her hair to tilt her head back just as my lips come down hard, cutting off her "What are you—" as I steal the breath right from her lungs.

I'm vaguely aware of the door opening next to us before slamming closed again. But I'm not quite ready to give up Kayan's mouth. I kiss her deep and thorough, and it's not until I feel her lower half grind against me that I know I should pull back, leave her wanting more of me in the hopes she'll stop fighting her feelings. Feelings I know she has. Feelings that match mine.

Kayan

"You can't just kiss people," I breathe, my body a melted pile of goo in his strong arms still holding me up, taking all of my weight.

Just then, July opens the door, and I stumble inside as

I try to get out of Z's embrace before she sees what we were doing on her front porch. I trip over the threshold, landing right where I started—wrapped up in Z's arms right before my face becomes one with July's floor.

"What's going on?" she asks. Is that a hint of amusement I hear in her voice?

I swat at Z's hands on my waist and stand to my full height before cocking my hip. "I came to make sure you were okay."

"Why wouldn't I be okay?" She frowns.

"I may have been frustrated about Z being at my house when I got home and told him about the guy coming to the hospital. I told him not to tell Wes, but no sooner did the words leave my mouth did this big lug call Wes." I stab a finger in Z's direction, but all he does is smile at me, the look traveling right to my lady bits, as I can still feel where his beard scratched at my tender face only moments before. He must be a mind reader or something, because his grin grows, and I glare. "You're annoying."

"You've said that, kitten," he reminds me, and I roll my eyes.

"You couldn't call?" Wes asks, taking his place beside July. From his disheveled appearance, I can tell we interrupted something. Good. Serves him right for his rudeness.

July backs me up. "Don't be rude."

"I'm hungry," is all he says, but I can tell he's most definitely not talking about food by the way my best friend's face turns a bright shade of red.

"I'm hungry too," I chime in.

"I was going to make tacos," she tells me, and then sighs.

"Do you have enough?" I question, begging her with my eyes not to send me off alone with the intoxicating man standing entirely too close to me.

"Yes," she states, at the same time Wes growls, "No."

"Yes, I have plenty," she reiterates, glaring at Wes as if daring him to say otherwise. "Why don't you help me make dinner, while Wes and Z do guy stuff?"

"Guy stuff." Wes shakes his head, looking over to his friend.

"Yeah, drink beer, scratch your balls... guy stuff," she says, her voice exasperated as she throws her hands in the air, rolling her eyes when Z laughs.

I swat him in the stomach with the back of my hand, but it hurts me more than him. "I'm going to start cooking," I state, rubbing my hand as I walk toward the kitchen.

Behind me, I hear Wes tell Z, "I'm beating the shit out of you tomorrow," and my suspicions we interrupted some hanky-panky are confirmed.

A few seconds later, July enters the kitchen, and we start to cook dinner.

"How much trouble did I get you in with Wes?" I ask with a wince.

"None. Well, he was pissed, but he got over it."

"I didn't mean to open my mouth, but when I got home, Z was there and it just came out," I confess.

"I kinda got that. What's going on with you guys anyway?" she asks, handing me two tomatoes to dice.

I duck my head, trying to hide the guilty look on my

face when I lie, "Nothing." I'm still not ready for her to know I slept with a guy I barely know.

"Didn't look like nothing when I opened my front door and his tongue was down your throat," she says gently, and my eyes widen. I must've been too consumed by his kiss to realize July had opened the door and seen us there.

"That was an accident," I chirp.

"He accidently kissed you? Or you accidently kissed him back?" she clarifies, and I shrug.

"I don't know." I sigh.

"He seems to like you."

He does. And I really like him too. But this is all happening so fast! I want to confide, but instead, I only whisper, "I don't know."

"I just don't want you to miss out on something great," she tells me after a few minutes of us silently preparing the food.

"He makes me crazy," I tell her, looking into my best friend's beautiful eyes.

"I think that if you don't explore things with him, you're going to end up regretting it," she implores, and I feel that statement deep in my soul. I know she's right. What I feel when I'm with Z, what I feel right in my very bones when he smiles at me, or kisses me. That's not just some regular old chemistry. I know in my heart it's a much deeper connection than anything I've ever experienced in my life, and I should probably stop fighting him off before I ruin my chances and finally push him away for good.

I don't say all this though. I give her a quiet, "I know

you're right," and look down at the pan in front of her, frowning. "I thought we were making tacos."

She gestures at the concoction she put together. "These are tacos. They're 'I don't want to wash a million dishes' tacos," she explains, and I see she's just dumped everything into one large container. I guess we'll be eating it like a taco salad, which is fine by me. It's all going in the same place anyway—my growling belly.

I laugh and shake my head at her, going back to chopping.

"Psst," July whispers conspiratorially, and I lift my eyes once more. "I thought you should know, Wes just told me something about Z that might soften you up a bit."

"Oh yeah? What's that?" I ask, moving closer to her so the guys won't hear us.

"When I asked Wes if you'd be safe with him, he told me they've been friends since they joined the Navy when they were eighteen. Said he was one of the best guys he knows. And call me crazy, but I kind of trust Wes. He seems to have a fine-tuned radar for trustworthy people."

I have to agree with that. After all, he's in love with best girl I've ever known.

Z

"So what happened with your girl after I called?" I ask Wes curiously, taking a drink of beer.

"What do you mean?" he questions.

"Did you tell her what we found out about the guy?" At his sideways look, I put my hands up defensively. "I only ask, because I'm not sure how much to tell Kayan. I was going to let you be the guinea pig. See how July reacted before I did the same with her wonder twin."

He chuckles, shaking his head. "Yeah, I told her some. She was being hardheaded as fuck, so I had to scare her a bit so she'd listen the fuck up."

"I see. And how did she react to your tough love?" I wince.

"Made her cry. Felt like shit, but it had to be done," he confesses, rubbing the back of his neck.

"What did you say exactly? Maybe I'll take a different approach. Don't think I could take seeing Kayan cry. Not after seeing her that way after that fucker broke into her house."

He eyes me but doesn't call me out on the clear feelings I have for her. "I told her that the person this young guy and his father are involved with—the one fighting the dogs he ends up bringing to her clinic—are drugging women until they have no idea what they're doing and put them on the street, only letting them quit prostituting when they are too broken to make them money."

I suck in a breath between my teeth. "That had to be a shocker. I'm sure she hadn't thought past the dogs being fought."

"No, she hadn't. But she did say that boy looked scared, terrified even, and could tell he was there to warn them because he didn't want the girls to get hurt. I told her his dad owns Momma's Country and is actually a good man. But over the last couple months, he's gotten mixed up with some bad dudes. I confessed we didn't know exactly what was going on, but that my guess is he owes the guys money." He takes a pull from his beer. "I ended up promising her I'd help the boy and his dad if I can. Her cousin and I are looking into what's going on."

"Well you know I've always got your back, brother. The sooner we catch these assholes, the sooner the girls can stop worrying about the dogs. Although I do like having a reason to hang around and protect Kayan all the time." I chuckle.

Wes shakes his head with a small smile. "Never seen you like this, man. Not in all the years I've known you. Such a tiny thing to bring down such a big man."

"What is it they say? Big things come in small packages? She packs quite the punch."

"Well, from what I've seen, she's a fighter. Have you told her about the kind of... stuff you're into?" He eyes me over his beer bottle before taking a swig.

"I haven't exactly hidden it. But I haven't come right out and had a conversation about it either," I tell him, and he nods.

"I can see it going one of two ways. Either it's going to speak to that sweet, submissive side I saw in her when y'all first met that night at Momma's Country, or her feisty side is going to come out and she's going to make you her bitch. Hope you've got lots of lube, bro." He cackles.

I join in his laughter, not hating the idea of Kayan being in control. What would it be like to let such a small morsel of a woman hold all the power over me in bed?

If what I'm feeling about her is anything to go by, it wouldn't be so bad. Wouldn't be so bad at all.

9

KAYAN

A few days later and it's the weekend. We've fallen into this surreal, happy routine, much to my surprise. I've held my sass in check after taco night at July's, even after finding Z in the same spot every evening when I get home from work—sprawled on my couch and watching TV.

The first day, I asked him—nicely—"Don't you work? How are you always here when I get home?"

"I'm a mechanic at the club's motorcycle shop. I make my own hours, so I'm able to get here a little while before you do to make sure it's safe for your arrival," he replied, and I instantly melted by the front door.

We've entered this getting-to-know you phase, and I actually really love it. He took it to heart when we got home from July's that night and I told him I needed to slow things down. Combined with my totally awkward rambling while we had sex that first time, when I was trying to cram information about him into my brain, all while he worked my body like he had a cheat code to all my secret buttons.

But the more I learn about him, the more I want him. To the point where I'm using my detachable showerhead —more than once—daily. His scent, his all-consuming presence, fills my little house, and I don't hate it. Not one bit. This place is back to being my safe space, all thanks to him.

We watch movies every night, discovering *The Fifth Element* is both of our favorite movie of all time. We quote it to each other randomly, even through texts while we're at work, and I giggle like a damn fool every time.

And not once has he pushed me to get physical again. I'll lay my head in his lap while we lounge on the couch, and he plays with my hair or scratches my back, but he never so much as tries to grope me.

And. It's. Making. Me. Crazy!

I know, I know. I'm annoying my damn self with my conflicting thoughts. I want to take things slow, loving that he's willing to do what I wish. But at the same time, all my body wants is to wrap around him and ride him like his damn Harley he forces me on. Which I also begrudgingly enjoy.

Everything inside me that's always been a defiant, impudent—let's face it—asshole since I moved out of my parents' house, where I was forced to play this annoying role of the perfect, rich princess, Z douses like he's a freaking fire extinguisher. And at first, when I found it super aggravating, I now admittedly love it. He's good for my blood pressure, it seems. And the more time we spend together, the calmer I feel inside my usually over-thoughtful brain.

The only thing I wish would change is his vagueness. While he doesn't mind answering any questions I have about his past and who he is as a person, he's super secretive about anything that deals with the motorcycle club or day-to-day happenings. He'll share all about work, what he had for lunch, stuff like that. But if ever he gets a call from one of his biker brothers—or so I assume—and has to leave for a few hours, he finds a way to change the subject. He's so perfect it makes me wonder: is that really who he says it is on the phone, or does he have some other chick he's running off to see?

I know that's just my past experience rearing its ugly head. But it really irks that part of me that has to know details. I can't help it; I'm a Virgo.

Tonight, there's a party at the compound. I'm excited to go, because maybe I'll be able to snoop a little, ask his friends some questions, and maybe they'll give me more information than what Z is willing to open up to me about. I mean, I don't think their club is into anything too bad. There's no way July would be okay with being in a relationship with someone who does illegal shit, and Wes seems to be a little more open with her than Z is with me. When I asked her about this, she chalked it up to Wes being the club president and not having to get approval from anyone else what information he divulges.

I've showered and put on my thong and bra, and am just inside my bathroom, blow drying my hair, when Z walks into the bedroom. He stops in his tracks when he sees me, bent over and blowing the underside of my hair dry. I watch him from upside down as he closes the door then leans back against it, crossing those huge arms over his chest and his feet at the ankles. His biceps bulge, the tattoos seeming to dance as they flex, bared for my viewing pleasure.

I can feel my knees tremble, wanting to buckle at the mere sight of him, but I force myself to play it cool, flipping my hair back as I stand up straight. Running the brush through my long strands, I face more toward him so he can have a view of my front, hoping he's admiring where the scalloped edge of my lace panties hugs me just right. Or are his eyes following the not-so-subtle wobble of my breasts as they practically spill over the top of my black push-up bra?

I refuse to look at him. I'm the one who said I wanted to take it slow, so now I must suffer the consequences. But I can feel his eyes on me, burning me even from the distance between us, and it makes my core melt for him. All I can do is hope that his control snaps. All he has to do is step in my direction and touch me. Just one skim of his hand along my flesh, and I will make it perfectly clear that this whole sex ban has been lifted.

Concentrating on my hair, the dryer is so loud I don't hear his approach. My heart thuds inside my chest as I first feel his overwhelming heat at my back, and then my eyes meet his in the mirror. Still, he doesn't touch me, and I bite my bottom lip for control. One step backward and I'd be pressed against his rigid muscles and hard planes.

Even with all the different fragrances in the bathroom —my shower gel, shampoo, and conditioner, then my coconut oil and lotion, plus the heat protection spray for my hair—it's his natural scent that now intoxicates my senses. I close my eyes and breathe it in, rocking back and forth on my feet as I continue blowing my hair.

Suddenly, the brush is taken from my left hand, and my eyes snap open just in time to watch Z take the dryer from my right, and all I can do is brace my hands on my vanity as he takes over the job. One corner of my lips quirks upward as his movements are awkward for the first few swipes of the brush, but clearly he'd been watching my technique, because he soon picks up the movement I always use. He drags the brush down the strands, the dryer chasing behind it, over and over until that section is smooth and no longer damp.

The tension builds to an unbearable level as he finishes up his work but still hasn't actually touched me. Just the air from the dryer and the occasional soft scrape of the brush's bristles along my scalp have graced my flesh. It drives me absolutely mad. My breath comes in sharp pants as I lean against the sink, and I startle when the dryer shuts off, the silence in the small room making my ears ring as he sets it on the vanity and unplugs it from the wall.

I chance a peek at him in the mirror, and his eyes blaze as they meet mine. His nostrils are flared, and the muscles in his arms are rigid. He stares into me as he pulls the brush through my locks, and I can't help but feel he's trying to tell me something with that look. No, not tell... ask. Maybe it's just my hopeful imagination, but it's as if I can hear that look pleading for permission. To do what, I don't know, but I answer it with a tiny nod, just in case I'm imagining things.

Clearly, I'm not, because the moment he sees that I granted him permission, his body goes lax for a split second before he takes the half a step forward and wraps his left arm around me, pulling me flush against his giant frame. I sigh in relief at the contact, and a shiver runs through me as he strokes the brush's bristles down my arm.

His arm bands around my ribs, pushing my breasts even higher in the black bra, and I watch his eyes flare in the mirror as he watches them move with each of my heavy breaths. He shifts to the left slightly, and the flesh he bares of my backside prickles with goose bumps. The bristles are dragged up over my right shoulder then halfway down my back before they stop, and I see his questioning look once more.

I'm not dense. I know Z is into some kinky shit. I've overheard Wes picking on him for it. But he didn't do anything crazy the first time we made love, and he hasn't tried anything since. So I don't know exactly what he's wanting to do to me with my black plastic paddle brush, but I do know I trust him with my life and that he'd never hurt me.

So again, I give him the little nod he's obviously waiting for.

Moving his left hand upward, he tilts my head to the right, moves my hair out of the way, and buries his face in my neck as he breathes me in, making me shiver in delight as his beard scrapes my sensitive skin there as the bristles of my brush do the same, going lower, and lower still, until he circles my exposed ass cheek. Just as he nips my neck between his perfect white teeth, I squeak and jump as he flips the brush around and swats my butt with the backside.

He glances in the mirror to see my reaction, and all he must see there is my flushed cheeks and the need in my eyes, because as he turns into my neck again, he strikes my ass once more, a little harder this time. I gasp at the sting, but as the prickly, hot sensation spreads up my spine and down my legs, I moan, the sound echoing off the bathroom walls.

"You like that, kitten?" he growls, and the vibration of his voice just adds to the already palpable tension surrounding us.

My whimper and frantic nod isn't enough. He rumbles, "I need your words, Kayan. I need you to tell me you're okay with this, and promise me you'll speak up if you don't like something." He circles the right globe of my ass with the brush as he waits for my response, driving my need even higher.

"I promise, Z. Plea—" I cut myself off. He didn't say he wanted me to beg, just that he wanted my promise. I've read enough dirty books and seen all the Fifty Shades movies enough to know not to do more or less than what a Dom specifically asks for, unless you want to be left high and dry, without an orgasm in sight.

But Z must not follow these rules, because he asks, "Please what, kitten? Tell me what you want."

I meet his eyes, not in the mirror, but by actually turning my head to look him in his gorgeous, chocolate orbs. "You, Z. All of you. I want you to do to me everything you desire. No holding back, worried I won't like what you do. Because I can guarantee, if you're the one doing it to me, I'm gonna like it. Like... really, *really* like it."

He closes his eyes and groans, and I feel the stinging swat of the brush against my ass cheek one last time before he tosses it in the sink and picks me up, carrying me to my bed.

Z wastes no time. He grasps my thong and tears it down my legs, diving forward and burying his face between my legs. I cry out in shock at the sensation that's just this side of too much as he sucks my clit between his lips, and he pulls back, looking up at me. "Did I hurt you?"

"No, it's just... I'm super sensitive," I confess, my cheeks flaming.

He props himself up on his elbows, glancing between my pussy then my eyes. "And why are you so sensitive, my little one?"

I shudder as he calls me his, even as my body grows hotter with embarrassment at being caught. "I... I used my... my showerhead while I was getting ready for the party."

He groans once again, this time against my now-throbbing core. "Thinking of what, kitten?"

My hips circle, enjoying the scratch of his beard between my thighs. "Not of what, Z. Of *who*. And it was you. Always. Fucking. You," I tell him, and that's all it takes. He opens his mouth and places it over my pussy, his hot breath soothing me for just a moment before he sucks my puffy lower lips, making my eyes roll back in my head as I scream his name.

He pulls back a moment to ask, "Does this mean you finally want to give this thing between us a chance? Do you want to give us a try?"

The hope in his eyes is my undoing. "Yes, Z. Dear God, yes. I don't want to fight it anymore. I just want you," I reply, and seeing that hope turn into joyous relief, I can't help but smile down at him.

He sets back to it, working my body like he wrote its

manual. His light laps at my clit and the gentle nibbles around my entrance drive me mad, to the point my eyes no longer see and my ears are ringing.

Ringing.

Ringing.

Wait...

That's not my ears ringing.

That's my freaking phone!

I sit up abruptly, but he doesn't stop his ministrations. I'm panting as I reach for my cell, where it's plugged in on my nightstand. July's name flashes across the screen, and I know she's wondering why we aren't at the party yet.

"Hello?" I answer breathlessly, just as Z does this magical thing with his front teeth, and I moan into the phone.

The connection goes dead, but I couldn't care less as he nibbles along my folds.

"Did you really just answer your phone in the middle of this, kitten?" he growls against me.

"I'm sorry. It's a compulsi— ohhhhh," I moan again, tossing my phone back on the nightstand as I grasp the back of his shaved head. "Please, Z. I need you."

He grants me mercy, standing up from the bed long enough to peel off his clothes in record time before grasping my ankles and flipping me over in one swift move. He takes hold of my hips and pulls me up on my hands and knees, placing a kiss where the brush must've left a pink mark on my right cheek. My skin prickles as he bites me there, my elbows almost buckling as he comes up on his knees behind me. Cock in hand, he runs it up and down my dripping slit, and when he's fully planted inside me, his big, rough hand slaps my left ass cheek, the sensation overwhelming my every sense as I buck against him.

"Oh, God! Yes, Z. More," I pant, lowering myself to my elbows and lifting my ass higher to his needed assault.

That's all he seems to want to hear, as he pounds into me and I'm suddenly lost in the glorious feeling of his cock filling me over and over while he slaps my ass, never in a pattern, so I can't anticipate his next move.

Soon, I'm screaming into my pillow, crying out with my orgasm as I try to breathe between squeals of pleasure. And with one... two... three more thrusts, and one last shaky squeeze of my hips as he holds me to him like a vise, I feel him spill inside me, his hot cum soothing the walls of my battered pussy.

He collapses to the side, taking me with him as he wraps me up in his giant arms. And the last thing I remember is giggling when he breathes into my hair, "Hell of a party."

10

Z

Time passes by in the blink of an eye. It's been weeks, maybe a month, since the night Kayan said she would give us a try, and it's been fucking perfect—well, almost. When her parents called one night, she put them on speakerphone—expecting me to join the conversation after what should've been a happy introduction—and told them about the man she was dating when her mother asked if she had met anyone since the last time they talked. From what I gathered, the answer to that question was usually a resounding no.

But instead of being happy she'd finally replied yes, they grilled her, trying to pull every detail about me out of her that they possibly could, so I stayed silent. Everything my kitten said in her proud and impressed voice that puffed up my chest seemed to dig me deeper and deeper into a hole of not good enough.

"He was in the Navy" was rebuked with "Oh, so he didn't go to college?" "He's a mechanic at a motorcycle shop" was reprimanded with "So he depends on commission. You don't want to live paycheck-to-paycheck, dear." Getting emotional, when she told them "He's protective and treats me like a queen," even I had to look away, my eyes feeling strange as they teared up for the first time in decades. Their response—"Of course he does now. But what about when he gets bored of you like all the others, darling?"—was the final straw. Cutting Kayan off before she could fire back, I calmly took the phone out of her hand and disconnected the call, ignoring the several tries her parents made to call her back.

After that night, making love to her until she forgot all about her parents, I came up with a plan. Which leads us to this moment, in my truck, driving across the North Carolina state line from our town in Tennessee. I'd show her exactly how someone should be treated by their parents, but before we made it to South Carolina, I had one stop to make, a treat for my kitten.

"Okay, I can't stand it anymore, Z. You've gotta tell me something," she whines, and I finally give in.

"We're making a pit stop near Ft. Vanter. My buddy from when I was in the military is part owner in a club there, and I want to treat you to a night out."

She tilts her head curiously. "A club? Like a dance club? Aren't we a little old for that?"

I chuckle. "No, kitten. Not a dance club."

"Ugh! Quit doing the vague thing. What kind of club is it?" she gripes.

I take a breath, hoping she doesn't react badly, because I really, really want to experience my friend Corbin's club with Kayan. Nothing on earth could possibly be better. "It's an alternative lifestyle club."

Her brows furrow. "An alternative lifestyle.... Z, honey,

call it what it is. You're taking me to a sex club, aren't you?"

Well, at least she isn't freaking out. "Technically, it's called a BDSM club."

She ponders this for a bit, pulling that sexy, full bottom lip between her perfect white teeth. Just when I start to fidget in my seat, she proclaims, "All right. I'm down. But I'm not getting naked in front of other people. I'm okay with taking in the scenery and stuff, but do not ask me to do the dirty in front of an audience."

God, I love this woman. If I didn't know it before, I do in this exact moment. I love Kayan down to my very soul.

"I'd never let anyone see what's only mine to enjoy, kitten. There are private rooms, and I promise no one will get even a peek at your beautiful naked body," I tell her, my voice low.

She blushes, tucking her hair behind her ear. "Okay," she murmurs, and she sits back in her seat, the look on her face clearly revealing all the thoughts in her mind about what going to Club Alias could be like.

We arrive in the small town next to Ft. Vanter, NC just as the sun sets and check into our hotel room. After grabbing some dinner, we pull into a spot in the parking garage beneath the building Club Alias is in. As I open Kayan's door, I can't help but admire how gorgeous she is in her simple little black dress she changed into. It fits her like a second skin, accentuating her round hips and small waist. It's got a high neckline, but her feminine curves can't be hidden. She's the most beautiful woman I've ever seen.

She grasps my bicep as we climb the few steps to street level, keeping herself steady in her high heels. I can tell she's nervous, but I don't try to soothe her. It just builds up the excitement of the experience. She's absolutely lucky that Club Alias will be the first BDSM club she'll ever attend. It's the best of the best in the whole country. The guys spared no expense when they built the place, filling the various private rooms with all the top of the line toys, tools, and devices.

Membership is hard to come by. The join fee is astronomical; plus, the application process weeds out anyone not worthy of a purely magical place such as this. I was lucky enough to be a founding member. Corbin contacted me as soon as he and his security team came up with the idea to open this place on the side. My join fee came with many perks the regular members weren't privy to. The important one tonight being that I can bring Kayan, who is not a member who's been through the crazy application process. Normally, she'd have to have at least four therapy sessions with Doc, the resident psychologist and leader of their security team. Once deemed safe as either a Dominant or a submissive, she'd have to go through training sessions with Seth for approval to use each and every one of the devices in the private rooms. Not to mention the five-figure join fee.

No, because I'm a founding member, I get to bring guests, because they trust me not to bring someone unfit into their establishment. They know I will uphold all the rules of Club Alias and not take advantage of my privileged standing with the guys, or it'd be an immediate loss of membership. And there was no way in fuck that'd happen. This is my own personal "happiest place on earth."

I open the unmarked, blacked out door and lead her

up the stairs that greet us, making sure to watch her face as the club comes into view the higher we climb. Her expression doesn't disappoint. Her eyes widen, her jaw drops prettily, and she takes in her surroundings with a look of wonder on her beautiful face.

Directly in front of us is a wide dance floor framed by luxurious leather booths. There are a couple bars with stools, where they serve every drink one could ever think of. Just above the booths, which have high backs for privacy, you can see the top of each private room. A few have their curtain drawn, but the glow of the open rooms beckons me to take Kayan into one and have my way with her.

"Do you want a drink first?" I ask her, and she looks up at me.

"Nah, I think I'm okay. I had the one glass of wine with dinner, and it didn't set very well, so I think I'll stay away from any alcohol tonight," she replies, and my brow lowers.

"Do you feel okay? If your stomach is upset, we can come back another time. Maybe on the way back from our trip to South Carolina?" I suggest. I don't want anything ruining her first time here. I don't want her to look back and only be able to remember that she felt like shit.

"Oh no, I'm fine, Z. That's why I chugged all that water before we left the restaurant. I promise I'm perfect," she assures, and I can't help the grin that spreads across my face.

"You're damn right about that, kitten."

She blushes and smacks my chest, shaking her head at me. "So what do you want to do first?" she asks, and her eyes move to a couple making out passionately in one of the booths. A moment later, another woman joins the couple, and as she takes off her shirt, Kayan's face flames once more and her eyes jerk to me. She looks relieved when she sees I only have eyes for her. "Hopefully not that," she murmurs.

"Never that. I'd never share you, not with a man nor a woman. You're all mine, Kayan. I mean that." I raise her hand to my lips and press a long kiss to her knuckles, watching her face go soft. I love that this is her reaction now, unlike before, when she seemed like she wanted to rebel against my claim on her. "I'd really like to show you what one of the private rooms is like. You game?"

"Most definitely," she purrs as my kiss moves from her knuckles to nibbling the tip of each finger.

I turn to lead her to Private Room #4, my personal favorite, when I almost run into someone, his arms crossed over his wide chest, black Henley pulled tight. But it's the mask he wears—a black leather executioner's hood—that's more ominous than anything.

"And who do we have here?" His deep voice resonates from behind the mask, and immediately, my entire body relaxes as a smile splits my mouth.

"Sarge," I say, and I stretch out a hand. I hear his chuckle as he takes it and pulls me into a hug with a loud slap to my back. When we step back, my arm circles Kayan's waist. "Sarge, let me introduce you to my woman. Kayan, this is my buddy from the military I was telling you about. While we're here, you'll notice most people wear masks in order to keep their identities secret. We have to use his Dom name, Sarge, while we're here as well."

"N-nice to meet you," she stutters, obviously thrown off by the hood. But still, she reaches her hand out and shakes his just as a very pregnant woman steps up beside him. Her mask is intricate and sparkling, the silver metal gleaming in the lights swirling around the dim dance floor. Corbin's arm wraps around the small of her back and pulls her into his side.

"Zar, you remember Vi?" my friend prompts, and I have to keep my own jaw from dropping. The last time I'd spoken to my friend, they were divorced after a pretty heartbreaking split. But if the look of possessiveness and infatuation on Vi's face are anything to go by, not to mention the round belly Corb was now stroking with his palm, they'd gotten a second chance at their life together.

"I do. And it looks like congratulations are in order," I reply, smacking my friend on his shoulder.

"This is number two, actually," Vi tells me. "It seems it's his goal to keep me knocked up forever. Our firstborn is still only a baby."

"Just making up for lost time, baby girl," he says low, pulling her closer and kissing the side of her head.

Vi practically melts against him, and I can't help but smile over at Kayan, who glances up at me with a look of love in her eyes.

"Well, I'm sure you two don't want to spend all your time chatting with us. Y'all are in Tennessee, right? Quite the trip you made, so we'll let you start your night," Vi says, taking Corbin's hand.

"Yep, near Nashville. Since my favorite place in the whole world is on the way to our destination in South Carolina, there was no way I couldn't stop and show it to my woman," I reply, and Vi smiles.

"Well I hope you enjoy your experience," she tells Kayan.

"I'm sure I will," she responds, looking up at me and wrapping her arm around my bicep.

Corbin reaches out to me once more, pulling me in for another man hug. "We'll catch up soon, man. Glad to see you've finally found the one," he says loud enough for only me to hear.

A few moments later, we're stepping inside my favorite private room, and I shut the curtain behind us. When I face the room, I see Kayan is walking around, taking in all the different equipment and devices we have the option to play with. My cock stirs as she reaches up to run her fingers through the tails of a flogger. She tilts her head to the side, a surprised look on her face. When her eyes meet mine, she says, "It's so soft. I expected it to be stiff with sharp edges."

"It's one of the reasons this place is the best. They don't skimp on their tools. Only the finest for Club Alias," I explain.

She moves to a cabinet, curiously opening the door and peeking inside. I stay where I am, watching her pick up and turn toys over in her hands as she studies them closely.

"And we can use whatever we want? No limit on how many we choose?" she asks.

This makes my dick stand at full attention. Not only does my girl want to be here, but she wants to make sure we can go all out and use as much stuff as we want. If I didn't think Kayan was my dream girl, I would now.

"Whatever you want, kitten," I growl, and it brings her

eyes to mine before they fall to my very noticeable erection tenting the front of my pants.

She bites her lip, and then raises her gaze to mine once more. "Here's the thing, Z. And I really hope it doesn't make you mad."

I take a step toward her, wanting to reassure her she can be completely honest with me. "What is it, baby?"

"I... I saw the people out there, being led around on leashes. I saw the masks, and the obedience, and the obvious power plays. I don't know if I'm ready for all that. Would... would you mind terribly if we just... have fun? I mean, from what I see in here, there's really nothing I wouldn't let you use on me if you wanted to. I trust you and know you won't hurt me. And I see quite a few things I wouldn't mind using on you. In fact, the thought is doing some funny things beneath my skirt," she admits with a giggle. "But as far as the like, bowing down and calling you by a 'Dom name'... I don't think I'd really be into that. In fact, I think I'd ruin it for you if I tried, because I wouldn't be able to help but laugh."

Dream. Fucking. Girl.

"Kitten, I don't need all that. I don't need you to kneel at my feet like I'm some kind of god. You already look up at me that way, whether you realize you do or not," I tell her, my heart pounding in my chest.

She crosses her arms and cocks a hip. "Is that supposed to be a short joke?" she accuses sassily, trying hard to conceal her smile.

I take another step toward her. "Nope, it's the truth. When you look up at me with those gorgeous eyes of yours, you already make me feel like I'm the king of the world, like I hung the moon and stars. I don't need you to role play or call me anything other than... yours."

Her arms lower, and her face goes slack. "Oh, Z. That's the sweetest thing you've ever said to me." Her bottom lip trembles.

I finally close the space between us then reach up to tuck her hair behind her ear before cupping her delicate jaw. "Just your willingness to try new things, to play with me and allow me to take you to places you've never been before, literally and figuratively, makes you my perfect partner. And I love you for it."

Her head jerks back and she seems to wobble on her heels, so I wrap my arm around the small of her back.

She squeaks a little, but doesn't form an actual word for a moment until she clears her throat. "I, uh. I'm a little confused," she states, and I smile, raising a brow in question. "Are you just saying like, 'I love this about you'? Or are you actually saying like, 'I love you'? Because there's a big difference. And my response to each of those statements is way different too."

I pull her even tighter against me, molding her to my front as I lean down to rumble in her ear, "I'm saying, kitten, that I love you. I love every single, solitary thing about you. But most definitely, I. Love. You."

I feel her nipples go hard as they poke into my abs, and she gives me her weight as she melts in my arms. "I love you too, Z."

My chest swells, and after kissing her thoroughly, I pull back to look into her eyes. "See? Happiest place on earth," I tell her, and she giggles.

11

KAYAN

We sleep in until checkout time at our hotel, and I wake up starving. I definitely worked off our dinner last night and then some, with all the different sexual adventures we tried at the club. I kind of feel sorry for the person who had to sanitize the room after us, because there wasn't a single surface or item we didn't use.

"What do you want to eat, kitten?" Z asks from the driver seat of his truck, and I think about it. Usually, I'm not one of those girls who takes a million years to decide what she wants to eat. I normally know exactly what I want for dinner, because I've been thinking about it since lunch.

"I'm thinking Bojangles' sounds good. But I'm not sure what to choose. Do I go with the pork chop biscuit with mustard? The sausage, egg, and cheese? Oo! Or maybe the country ham biscuit. That sounds good. But damn, it's salty. Whatever I get, I need to get a Bo-Berry biscuit for dessert. So maybe the gravy biscuit for my main meal," I ramble.

Z looks over at me funny. He's used to me being decisive with my food choices as well.

"Everything sounds good, so it's hard to choose," I defend. "And you know damn well I can't pass a Bojangles' without stopping for a Bo-Berry biscuit." After a silent moment... "This is *your* fault. You're the one who made me work up such an appetite."

He grins. "Whatever you want, kitten," he says, taking the next exit, which has a Bo not even a mile off the highway.

Two and half hours later—interrupted by a stop at a gas station, because I got super car-sick after the amount of food I devoured—we pull into a driveway out front of the most adorable one-story house surrounded by gorgeous oak trees.

I wasn't nervous about meeting Z's family until this exact moment. I had spent so much time talking to July, calming her down and telling her what a wonderful step it was that Wes wanted to introduce her to his mom that I hadn't really thought about it myself. And all July's worries hit me at once.

Is this too soon?

Are we moving too fast?

It seems like we've known each other for years, but in reality, it's only been a short time Z's been in my life.

Is his mom going to hate me?

Is she going to be like my parents, all judgmental of who I've picked to call mine?

And what about his dad? Z is intimidating enough as

it is. What would it be like being around him *and* the man he probably got his burliness from?

"They're going to love you," Z breaks into my thoughts, either reading my mind or the look of pure terror on my face.

"How do you know that? Do they love all the chicks you bring home?" I question with a roll of my eyes.

He reaches over and tugs my chin until I'm looking into his hypnotizing eyes. "I've never brought a woman home to meet my parents before, kitten. I just know."

"You've..." My chin wobbles against his knuckle. "You've never..." My lip trembles as tears swell in my eyes without spilling over. "I'm the first girl you've ever brought home? Like *ever*?"

His brow furrows. "Yeah, Kayan. You're the only one who's ever been worthy to meet them. They're the best people I know in this world. Well, before I met you, of course." My tears spill over and I sniffle, letting out a noise that's a cross between a sob, a laugh, and a very unladylike cough. "What's got you so emotional, baby?"

As he swipes my tears, I turn my face to press into his palm. "I don't know. I've just never felt this way about anyone before. And to know you feel the same way about me... it's just overwhelming. In a good way though. These are happy tears. I promise."

He gives me a sexy, slow smile that makes my heart skip a beat and my tears stall. "Fair enough. I love you. Now, let's get you inside."

I let out a dreamy sigh, most of my boiling fear about meeting his parents simmering down to low heat. "I love you too, Z. Let's do this."

As I release my seat belt, I pull down his visor and look in the mirror, swiping the evidence of my emotional state away. I'm glad I hadn't bothered with makeup today or I'd be a hot mess. Z opens my door just as I flip the visor back up, and I let him help me down from the high seat.

Before we even get halfway up the walkway, the door opens and a tall woman with gorgeous black hair and the best tan in history rushes out onto the wraparound porch. She's wiping her hands on a dishtowel, but tosses it to the ground as she suddenly takes off in a sprint toward us.

I let go of Z's hand, scared I'll get knocked over if she takes a flying leap into his arms. But to my surprise, it's me she's suddenly encircled her entire long, lithe body around like a praying mantis around a branch. I feel like, if I weren't so short in comparison, her mile-long legs would join the rest of her in cocooning me.

"Ma," Z nudges gently.

"Give me a minute, boy," she says at the top of my head, where her cheek rests.

She smells like cookies and light perfume, and even though I'd normally find hugging a complete stranger really awkward, all I feel is comfort radiating from her and into my very soul.

"Ma." Z tries again, a little more sternly this time, but it's me who swats blindly at him.

"Zzzzz. I'm super green, babe," I tell him.

He chuckles. "Quoting our favorite movie. You *must* be good." He clears his throat. "Thought you weren't a hugger though. Gettin' kinda jealous here."

With a chuckle, his mom unfurls and turns toward him. When she hugs him, her long arms barely make it all the way around his hulking form, but she's not too shy of being as tall as him. "There's my little boy." Her hand comes up to rub his shaved head and he turns his face against her shoulder to look at me, grin, and roll his eyes. I can't help but giggle.

"Louisa," a deep male voice comes from the porch, and I turn to see a very handsome older man bent down, picking up the dishtowel she'd dropped. "Let our boy breathe."

Ah, this must be Z's dad, and I try to keep the shocked look off my face as he comes down the front steps and makes his way toward us. I was wrong. So, so wrong. Z obviously got his stature from his mom, because I can almost look this man in his eye. He can't be more than 5'5", but goodness he is good-looking.

When Z's mom finally lets him go, she steps back and allows his dad a turn, and it's not one of those man-hugs with a slap on the back. It's a full on, loving hug from a father to his "little boy," only Z towers over him and rests his cheek on the top of his head the way Louisa did to me.

I've taken in every detail of this exchange since the woman had opened her front door, because it's so different from what happens whenever I go home for a visit—which is a very, *very* rare occasion. There are no loving hugs. Only cold greetings and the usual questions of when I'll meet a man worthy enough to be part of our hoity-toity family.

Z lets go but puts his hand on his dad's shoulder and gives it a squeeze as he faces me. "Kayan, this is my dad and mom, Mateo and Louisa Del Castillo. Ma, Pop, this is my Kayan."

My Kayan. He introduced me to his parents as *his* Kayan.

My nose tingles with tears wanting to form once again, but I fight them with all my might. I will not cry in the first five minutes of meeting these people. How freaking embarrassing would that be?

"It's nice to meet y'all," I squeak out, my throat tight with trying to keep my emotions under control.

His dad reaches out and tugs his wife into his side, wrapping his arm around her hips with possession and pride. Her arm comes to rest around the top of his shoulders, and she places a kiss on the top of his bald head. I feel my cheeks pinken. No way would my parents be caught dead showing any kind of PDA.

"It's truly wonderful to meet you, honey. Eleazar has talked about you nonstop, and we feel like we already know you," she says, her face soft and warm as her voice.

I glance up at Z, and he gives me an infectious smile.

"Anyway, let's get you two inside. I'm sure you're over being on the road after making that trip," his dad tells us, and we follow them up the porch steps.

"It really wasn't bad, since we split the trip in half last night," Z informs, and my eyes widen as I shake my head at him. He's not going to tell them about Club Alias, is he? He gives me a wicked grin like that's exactly what he's going to do, but to my relief, he only explains, "We stopped next to Ft. Vanter to see an old buddy of mine. Got some good sleep at a hotel last night before finishing up the trip."

"Ah, how nice. Anyone we know?" his mom asks.

"Corbin Lowe. He was in the Army while I was in the Navy. I got to train with him for a few months back in the day. Good guy." We walk into the kitchen, and he pulls a stool out at the island for me to sit at. I've been sitting for almost three hours now though, so I just prop my foot up on one of the rungs. "Are those what I think they are, Ma?"

I follow his gaze to the rack of cookies cooling in the center of the island.

"If you think they're you're favorite chocolate chunk and pecan cookies, then you are most certainly correct. But I just pulled them out, so you need to wait so you don't burn—"

But it was too late. Z already snatched up one of the cookies in his big hand, tossing some that fell apart into his mouth, making garbled noises and breathing in and out trying to cool the hot treat.

"Hardhead," his mom and I say in unison, and after a startled glance between us, we both burst into laughter.

"Well… there we have it," his dad inserts.

"*Wha*?" Z asks, his mouth full but open as he continues to eat the blistering cookie.

"They say a man unconsciously tries to find a woman who reminds them of their mother. And the same with a woman and her father," he explains, and I let out a snort by accident.

When they look at me, I try to smile, but it feels more like a grimace. "I think I consciously looked for someone who was the complete opposite of my father. Let's just say I wasn't a daddy's girl."

"Aw, honey. Eleazar was telling us about your parents. But you wanna know a secret?" His mom looks at me soothingly but without pity, and then glances at Z, as if asking for permission. At his nod, she continues. "Biologically, we are not Z's parents. We adopted him when he was ten."

My face shows pure shock, and the three other people in the room chuckle. "But you look so much alike!"

"That's because they adopted me from Ma's sister. Crazy, truly messed up situation back in Spain. But that's a story for another day. Who I call my parents—" He gestures to the couple smiling warmly at me. "—had tried for years to have a baby, with no luck. When I was about to be sent into foster care because of my biological mother and father, Ma and Pop saw it as the perfect opportunity to finally add to their family."

I nod, something in his eyes causing me to reach out and take Z's hand in mine. "It's why I've always understood your fucked up relationship with your parents. Because that's all I knew for the first decade of my life. The coldness. The feeling of being unloved, unworthy. It was terrible. But then I was adopted by who was truly meant to be my parents. And that's why I told you I'd bring you here, to show you how parents should treat their child. Because I knew both sides of it—how it's not supposed to be, and exactly what a family should be like."

"But no fear, Kayan!" she exclaims. "You have us now too. I will gladly be your doting, loving stand-in mom. We'll exchange numbers before you leave, and you can call me whenever you want."

"Don't do it," Z stage-whispers, and I glance at him with wide eyes. "Once you get on the phone with her, you can't escape. The woman loves to talk about anything and everything, or nothing at all."

Next thing I see is an oven mitt connecting with my

handsome hulk's face, and I turn to look at his smirking mother. "Nice shot," I tell her, and she gives me a single nod before narrowing her eyes on Z.

"I resent that. First, my only child leaves me to join the Navy and travel all over the world as soon as he turns eighteen, and then he settles states away when he gets out of the military. What's a mom to do? You bet your ass I'm gonna make you talk to me on the phone as much as possible," she tells him, her Spanish accent thickening the more she spoke, but she never slipped out of English.

I lean into Z, and murmur, "I totally expected her to start cussing you out in her native language."

He smiles down at me warmly. "Nah, she thinks it's rude to speak Spanish in front of people who won't understand what she's saying. Plus, she's just showing off in front of you, so she wants to be perfectly clear."

This time, it's a magenta potholder that hits Z upside his head, and I can't help but laugh loudly.

"I think I love your mom," I say, as every ounce of nervousness leaves my system.

THAT EVENING, I walk into the kitchen after lying down in Z's old bedroom for a nap. One minute, I was perfectly fine, hanging out with him and his parents in their living room. The next, it felt like someone had covered my nose with a chloroform rag and if I didn't go lie down that instant, I would pass out right then and there on the couch. Which made no sense, since we'd slept in this morning.

"Feeling better, sweetheart?" Louisa asks when she spots me.

"A little. Groggy, but I should be fine if you happen to have some coffee," I tell her, a hopeful look on my face.

"Of course. Right there in the corner is my coffee bar. Help yourself to whatever you like." She points, and that's when I notice the cutest little setup. She has a Keurig with a spinning wrack of all sorts of flavored K-cups sitting on a black iron buffet. On the wall are paintings of different mugs of hot drinks, and a sign that says **I like my sugar and cream with a hint of coffee.**

I choose one of the donut shop coffees, and see there's a black mini fridge built into the buffet, and when I open the small door, I giggle at all the different flavors of creamers. "You're really prepared for anything, aren't you, Mama Louisa?"

"Never know which coffee I'm going to be in the mood for, so I keep everything stocked," she tells me with a wide smile, probably at my use of the name she'd ordered me to call her when I referred to her as Mrs. Del Castillo earlier.

After I'm finished stirring in a not-so-healthy amount of peppermint mocha creamer, I sit at the island and sip from the mug for a minute before finally asking, "Where is Z? And do you need any help fixing dinner? It all smells amazing."

"I sent him and his dad on a mission to get flour tortillas to go with dinner tonight. I only have corn ones, and he informed me that you don't like them."

"Oh, gosh. Y'all didn't have to make a fuss about that. I would've been fine with corn tortillas. It's just a texture thing, no big deal," I say, my face heating. The last thing I want is for her to think I'm some ungrateful, picky asshole.

"No fuss at all, honey. Don't you worry about it. I personally thought it was sweet that he knew such a minor detail about your food preferences." She smiled, stirring something in a silver pot on the stove.

"It is really sweet. He learned that tidbit a short while ago, when we had taco night at my best friend July's house. I can't believe he'd remember such a random thing," I tell her, taking a sip of my coffee and moaning quietly at how it zings through my veins, waking me more with every swallow.

She chuckles, shaking her head and making her long, dark hair sway against her back. "My boy will surprise you. He's always been a good listener, and he gives the best gifts. You'll mention you'd like something in passing, and next holiday or birthday, there it is!"

"That seems like a rare quality in a man. You did good with him. He's the most thoughtful, caring, and protective man I've ever met."

Her eyes go soft as she turns to look at me, leaning on the counter next to the stove. "He actually gets it from his father, so it's a learned behavior, not nature. Mateo is the same way. And hopefully, your children will pick it up from Eleazar, especially if it's a boy. I'd much rather that trait be passed down through the generations than anything else. Things like looks and... height—" She winks. "—do not matter as much as how they treat you. But we shall see, yes?"

My cheeks warm at the idea of having babies with Z. I can already tell he'd be an amazing father, what with the way he's so protective and how he dotes on me. But I say, "We've still got a while before we even start thinking about babies. We only began dating a month or so ago."

Amusement fills her eyes and she cocks her head. "Oh, honey. I think God may have other plans for you and my boy."

I sit up straighter on the stool, setting my coffee mug down. "What do you mean?"

She comes to stand on the other side of the island, bending her tall form to rest her elbows on the countertop and looking me in the eye. "Darling girl, I would bet my entire life savings that you are carrying my first grandbaby right now, as we speak," she tells me, and I unconsciously back up on the stool, nearly falling off before I catch myself.

"Wh-what? Why would you say that?" My tone is more accusatory than questioning.

She comes around the island and pulls out the stool to my right, taking hold of my knees to swing me around to face her before taking my hands gently in hers. Her face is soft when she points out, "You said earlier that on the way here, you got carsick."

"Well, yeah. I ate too much at Bo—"

"And Eleazar was picking on you for being emotional when that commercial came on the TV, and asked if it was getting close to... Shark Week, did he call it? Ugh." She shakes her head.

"I mean, I am close. My periods have never been regular, even on birth control, but I should be starting any day," I murmur, a little weirded out I'm talking to my boyfriend's mom about my menstrual cycle on the same day I just met her.

"And then you got super sleepy all of a sudden, when you said you normally don't take naps during the day. Especially since you slept in this morning," she adds.

"When my best friend Jamie got pregnant, I swear she was narcoleptic. She could practically fall asleep on her feet. During her first trimester, she almost fell asleep driving home! It was quite crazy."

My eyes move between hers as I put all of these things together. Individually, I could explain them away. But when I look at them as symptoms pointing at one ailment... she's exactly right.

"Oh, shit," I breathe, and she grins widely. "Oh... oh, *shit*!"

She pats my knee, stands, bends to kiss my forehead, and then I watch numbly as she walks back around the island to where her phone is charging next to the stove. I watch, my mouth hanging open, as she dials someone then lifts the phone in front of her as she relaxes back against the counter.

"Hello, my handsomest son."

She has him on speakerphone, because I can hear his response of "I'm your only son, Ma. What did you forget? We're still at the store."

"I think your little kitten might need you to grab something for her while you're there," she replies, and winks at me with a soft smile.

"Is she up from her nap? Is she okay? Need some type of medicine?" His voice holds worry, and I feel warmth spread through me, lessening some of my shock.

"Here, I'm handing her the phone," his mom says, and she does just that.

"Kayan, you okay, baby?" he asks, and I shake my head slightly, forgetting he can't see me. "You there, kitten?"

"I... I, uh..." I can't form words.

His voice grows firmer. "Kayan, what's wrong?"

I jump when Louisa places her hand on my shoulder, giving it a squeeze in support. "I, uh... Don't be mad, okay?"

"Baby, have I ever been mad at you?" he prompts, and I shake my head again.

"N-no. But... but we've only been together—"

"I won't be mad. Just tell me what's the matter," he urges, and I take a deep breath.

"I, um. Would you mind grabbing a-uh.... Would you mind grabbing—"

"Ah, I get it. There's nothing to be embarrassed about, baby. I know we've only been together a short while, but I know how the female body works. I knew you were being extra emotional. Which do you need? Tampons or pads? Or do you use one of those weird cup things? I'm heading to the feminine products aisle now. I got this. You think anyone's going to look at me cross when I rock up to the register with plugs, chocolate, and wine for my girl? Fuck no," he carries on, obviously trying to make me laugh and soothe any embarrassment I might've had if I started my period and needed girly products. It makes me love him even more, and it's much easier this time when I speak.

"No. No, that's not it, Z. I... I need you to grab me... to grab *us*... a pregnancy test."

I hear his boot squeak he comes to such a sudden stop. His breath comes out in a whoosh, and then his voice is deep and quiet, way different than his jovial tone only moments ago. "You got my baby in you, kitten?"

It sends chills up my spine and down my arms, raising the hairs there. My face heats. "Your mom seems to think so," I murmur.

"The nap, the indecision about food this morning, the carsickness. On top of all the crying. Not to mention last night at the club, when your tits were too sens—"

"Z! You're on speaker! Just get the damn test, okay?" I cut him off, and I glance up wearily to find Louisa silently laughing behind her hand.

"No problem, baby. We'll be home shortly. And Kayan?" His voice gentles.

"Yeah, Z?" I squeak out.

"I love you. More than I can put into words. Nothing would make me happier than if you were carrying my child. I promise you that," he assures, and I feel ninety-five percent of my worry leave my body.

The other five percent has nothing to do with me, and everything to do with what my parents and best friend are going to say if the test ends up being positive.

12

Z

"**S**ilver," Jax calls, walking into the shop through the open bay's door.

We've been back from South Carolina for a week now, and it's been business as usual at our motorcycle shop. The only difference in my day is Kayan and I aren't even pretending we don't live together anymore. Since I only had a room at the MC's compound, it was easy to decide that I'd move in with her.

I see Wes lift his chin and step away from the bike he's working on while wiping his hands on a greasy rag.

"I have some news about Snake," Jax says, and my eye twitches at the mention of that fucker's name. I know Wes doesn't like to get involved with shit that isn't directly affecting the club, but we really don't have a choice. They got us involved the minute that boy dropped off one of their fighting dogs at our women's vet clinic. "He was seen leaving a meeting in downtown Nashville this afternoon."

"And?" Wes prompts

"And the meeting was with Franco Demitrez."

"Is that supposed to mean something to me?" Wes leans against the bike he was working on.

"He controls one of the largest sex trafficking and prostitution rings this side of the Mississippi," Jax tells him, and that gets my undivided attention. I set down my socket wrench and turn fully toward them. We had known it was probably pretty bad what Snake and his men were up to, but this takes it to a whole other level.

"You know I hate asking you for any favors," Jax begins, and I can't help but chuckle. He'd been asking us for favors since we'd known him. "I need you and your boys to see if you can set up a buy from him."

"Then what? Do you even know the level of fucked-up you're dealing with right now? You can't just set up a buy with guys like these, and you sure as fuck need to have a plan in place for when it's all over," Wes explains.

"I understand that. I also understand that my clients' eighteen-year-old daughter went missing two days ago. It looks like she ran away with her boyfriend, but my clients swear to me that's not the case and she would never do anything like that."

"Fuck! Was the boyfriend in on it?" Wes questions.

Jax fidgets then nods. "Yeah, the boyfriend's dad is one of Snake's new boys."

"Jesus," Wes hisses, disgusted. "Let me talk to my boys. I'll call you so we can meet up and figure out what we're going to do."

"I'm in," I say, going to Wes's side. I don't need to even think about it. I'm ready for this shit to be over with so I can stop worrying about these assholes fucking with my woman.

"Me too," Mic chimes in.

"I'm down," Harlen mutters.

"I was getting bored anyway." Everret shrugs, walking up to the group.

"Looks like we're in," Wes sighs. "We'll meet tonight and go over the details, but right now, I think this should just be a rescue mission. Once we have your clients' daughter safe, we'll figure out how to close the operation down."

"Until tonight," Jax says, heading out.

"We're going to need to get some weapons," I say.

"I know a place," Harlen tells us. "If I head out now, I should still be able to make the connect.

"Mic, you go with Harlen. Everret, you find out everything you can on Franco Demitrez."

"On it," Mic agrees, walking away, followed by Everret and Harlen.

"We're going to need someone to watch the girls," I tell Wes, and I run a hand over my head then look at him.

"I know. Maybe one of July's cousins can stay with them."

"Would they kill to protect them? Die to protect them?" I ask.

He thinks about it for a moment. "They would do whatever is necessary," he assures me.

"I wasn't going to tell anyone, not yet, 'cause it's so early, but Kayan's pregnant," I tell him quietly. "We weren't planning on this happening. Hell, I wasn't even planning on her." I rub my hand down my face, and when my eyes meet his, Wes is looking at me funny, his eyes almost soft and small smile on his face.

"Jesus, you move fast," he mutters, his smile widening.

"When she told me she was pregnant, I thought I was going to fucking pass out right there in the grocery store. I have never been so scared in my life." I shake my head, glancing away for a moment before looking at him again. "I never put much thought into the future until her," I confess, and it's the absolute truth. I lived day to day, not thinking about much, until that crazy, gorgeous girl stumbled into the bar wearing a catsuit. And then everything changed.

"I'm happy for you, brother." He pulls me in for a hug then leans back just enough to look me dead in the eye, wrapping his hand around the side of my neck with a grin. "You ever think two years ago this would have happened?"

"Fuck no." I shake my head and he lets me go.

"Me, neither." After a beat, he asks me, "You okay?"

He probably sees the slight worry on my face, so I explain, "Never been in love. You know my family is fucked up." We've had many nights, drinking and sharing parts of our lives not many people know. Wes is my best friend. There's nothing I don't share with him. Including everything about my biological parents, and how my aunt and uncle adopted me when I was a kid. "Before Kayan, I didn't even know what love felt like. Romantic love, I mean."

What I told Kayan is one hundred percent true. I am in this. I've never been happier in my life. Nothing is better than knowing the woman I love has my baby inside her. But at the same time, I'm terrified. What if my genetics somehow take over and I'm the worst father on the planet? My own parents didn't want me or care about me. They didn't care about anything besides the fucking drugs they loved more than their own child.

"I worry I won't do her justice," I admit, rubbing my chest.

"That's love, brother. Knowing you're not good enough, but keeping her anyways—that's love," he tells me.

"That's fucked up."

He laughs and agrees, "Yep."

13

KAYAN

"I want to follow Z tonight," I say as July locks the doors to the clinic.

I keep telling myself it's my hormones messing with my mind, but now I'm obsessing. Completely. Obsessing. And if I don't get answers, I'm going to have a mental breakdown.

"Follow him where?" July asks, and I pull my keys out of my bag.

"I don't know," I murmur then look at my best friend. The best friend I don't deserve. What kind of woman doesn't tell her best freaking friend she's pregnant the millisecond she finds out? And it's been a week! But I shove that aside and confess, even though it sounds absolutely stupid, even to my own ears, "I feel like maybe he's cheating. He's been hiding something."

She frowns at me. "I don't think Z is cheating on you."

"Tonight, I'll find out for sure," I say, and she knows there's no talking me out of it.

When we were in college, I dated a guy who was cheating on me. The whole time, everyone knew except for me and July. Well, that was until we went to a frat party and walked in on him while he was having sex with our other roommate, Lynn. The fucking whore.

"Well, I'm going to go with you," July tells me.

See? That's how a real best friend treats their girl. Not like me and my secret-having ass. First, I kept having sex with Z from her. And now I'm keeping my pregnancy from her. What the hell is wrong with me? Did my parents really fuck me up that much? I need to find a way to tell her. But for right now, all I say is, "Thank you."

"I always have your back, even if I think you're crazy," she tells me, making me feel even more guilt.

"We're going to have to find some way to ditch our tail." I nudge my chin toward Harlen, who is sitting on his bike across the parking lot.

"The anniversary edition of *Fifty Shades of Grey* comes out tonight. We will just say we're going to watch it."

"Perfect," I whisper.

"Call me and we'll make plans for the movies!" she shouts loud enough for Harlen to hear.

"I can't wait to see Fifty's ass on the big screen!" I shout back, and she laughs genuinely.

Standing next to Z's bike, I watch as July's cousin Sage pulls into the parking lot with her in the passenger seat. It was nearly impossible to convince Z that I needed to take my car, but when I finally broke out the big guns —"I'm just really scared to get on your bike, when I have our little bun in the oven"—he finally gave in.

"Hey, Z, are you sure you don't want to watch the

movie with us?" she asks, hopping out of Sage's truck and skipping over, looking super excited to see the movie. When in reality, I'm sure she's just super hyper from anxiety. It's always me who drags her on these "adventures."

"Thanks, but no, thanks." He smiles then turns and kisses me. He holds me in his arms, whispering in my ear for only me to hear, "I love you, kitten. Eat all the snacks you want, but stay away from chocolate. I read on the internet today that chocolate and tomatoes could be the culprit for your reflux and nausea. I'll grab you some Zantac on my way home just in case you can't resist though."

My heart breaks. What the hell am I thinking? How could I possibly believe my man is cheating, when he's spending time during his day looking up remedies for my pregnancy symptoms?

But he's still so freaking secretive. Still gives me incredibly vague responses when I ask him about his day. I just have this feeling he's hiding something from me. And maybe it's my past relationship that's causing the mistrust, which is totally unfair to Z, but he isn't doing anything to help me past it with all his ambiguous responses to my questions.

"Let's go." July smiles, threading her arm through mine, and we head to the theater, Sage following close behind us.

"Are you sure you don't want to come in?" she asks her cousin before we make it to the ticket counter.

"Nah, I'll wait here," he replies, and we turn to pay for our tickets. We stop to get popcorn and candy—I grab Sour Patch Kids instead of my usual chocolate-covered almonds—and give Sage a final wave before heading into the movie.

"What's the plan?" I ask as we walk into our theater.

"We go out the backdoor to your car," she tells me, leading me toward the front of the theater, where she pushes through the door marked *Exit*. The moment we clear the door, adrenaline hits me and my heart starts to pound wildly in my chest as we head down the walkway to the side parking lot where my car is parked.

It's probably why I overreact and shriek, "What are you doing?" as July starts to toss the food we got into the garbage that is on the corner of the building. "You cannot throw that out." I pull the popcorn from her hand forcefully, making half of it land on the ground, and I pout. "Or this." I hand her the keys to my car and take the soda from her. I've been staying away from it for the past week, but it's only Sprite, so it's caffeine free.

"Are you good now?" she asks.

I shrug and take a swig, and she rolls her eyes then starts making her way to my car. The whole time, I glance around to make sure Sage isn't anywhere around. Once we get it unlocked and us buckled inside, July starts up the car and pulls out of the parking lot toward the compound.

"So much for this plan," I grumble through a mouthful of popcorn as we pull up in front of the compound fifteen minutes later. I toss in a green Sour Patch Kid for good measure.

"Yeah," she agrees. The next thing I know, July is shoving my head down and ducking, and that's when I hear the sound of a motorcycle pulling up. When the roar cuts off, we lift our heads and watch Harlen walk inside, coming out minutes later carrying an envelope.

"We need to follow him. He will be with Z," I whisper, as if he could hear us inside the car from this far away.

"I know," she murmurs, and we follow him down back roads for what seems like forever. When he pulls into a parking lot, July parks a block away, and we watch as he rides right to where the rest of the guys are waiting. When he gets off his bike, he says something to Wes then hands him the envelope. Even from this distance, we can see Wes is obviously pissed. He puts his phone to his ear.

"I wonder what they're talking about," I mumble.

"I don't know," she replies.

Wes goes over to Z and pats his arm, saying something to him, and my brow furrows. When Z's body goes rigid, nausea overtakes my system.

"We're busted," I whisper. I don't know how I know, but I do. July looks at me, puts the car in drive, and takes off. The moment we hit the main road, the sound of motorcycle pipes fills the air. "Oh my God. Z is going to kill me." I brush the popcorn mess off my boobs nervously.

"Maybe we can get back to the theater," July tells me, but from the look on her face, I can tell she doesn't even believe that herself.

"Yeah, maybe," I agree, already planning my own funeral. I think I'd like my casket covered in hydrangeas. I bet that'd be pretty.

I press back in my seat as July accelerates and takes back roads all the way to the theater. The moment she turns off the car, we get out and rush toward the door we left out of, but then stop dead when we come face-to-face with a visibly fuming Sage.

"Hey, what are you doing out here?" July asks, her voice three octaves higher than normal.

His eyes flare with rage. "Are you fucking kidding me?"

"What? I came out to smoke. You know... the scenes were so hot I needed a cigarette," she says, and I have to force myself not to slap my own forehead. God, I love my best friend. We hear someone chuckle, and we both turn to look as Mic, Wes, Z, and Jax walk up to where we're standing.

"This shit's not funny," Wes growls, glaring at Mic, who holds up a hand defensively in front of him.

When Wes's eyes meet July's, they do one sweep then he looks at Sage.

"You mind taking the girls home? We'll be there in an hour."

"No problem, man," Sage answers.

I don't have it in me to meet Z's eyes. I'm not ready to face his wrath quite yet.

"Do not fucking leave the house." Wes points at July, and it only adds to my guilt. I'm always getting my poor bestie in trouble. What the hell is wrong with me?

"Give me your keys," Z orders me. I jump at the anger in his voice and grab July's hand. I turn to look at her, my nose tingling as tears fill my eyes. She hands the keys over, and I watch as Z storms off toward the parking lot.

"We—" July starts, but her man cuts her off.

"Do not fucking talk," Wes says, and I hear July's teeth click as her mouth slams shut. "I'll deal with your ass when I get home."

At that, I feel her hand tighten around mine as anger overtakes all her other emotions, but she holds it in check, not saying anything in response.

"Let's go," Sage tells us, and leads us away from the guys and toward his truck.

"Sorry about leaving," July mumbles from the passenger seat.

"You know we wouldn't be watching you guys if there wasn't some fucked-up shit going on," Sage replies, and it makes my brows furrow. Why won't anyone tell us what the hell is going on? When we get to July's, Sage shuts off his truck, and we follow him to the front door before she lets us inside. "Both of you, sit here," he growls, pointing at the couch.

July turns her glare on her cousin like a laser beam, and he visibly flinches.

"First, we're not going to leave again, and second, I'm older than you and this is my house. Now, if you don't mind, I'm going to take my friend back to the bathroom so she can splash some cold water on her face!" she shouts, and then we turn and she tugs me to the hall bathroom. "Sit here," she tells me, closing the lid on the toilet so I can take a seat, and then she grabs a washcloth and runs it under the water before handing it to me.

"Thanks," I murmur, pressing it to my face.

"He's not cheating," comes her sweet voice, and I exhale, squeezing my eyes tight. With all the craziness of the last forty-five minutes, the thought hadn't even crossed my mind. But she's right. Z wasn't sneaking off with some other woman. He was sneaking off with his biker club brothers. So why couldn't he just talk to me about it? Doesn't he trust me? Does he think I'll rat him out if he's doing something illegal? I mean, I wouldn't be happy about that, if that's what he's doing. But I love him. I'm carrying his child. I wouldn't do anything to get him in any kind of trouble.

When we go back out to the living room, Sage is watching television. "The guys are on their way back."

"Great," she mumbles, and my nausea returns.

When the sound of their motorcycles rumbles outside, I nearly vomit right there in the living room.

The front door flies open, and my heart skips a beat when I see it's Z busting in like he owns the place.

"How the fuck do you think it's okay to take a pregnant woman on one of your crazy-ass adventures?" he roars at July, and all the blood drains from my face. I swallow bile rapidly, trying to keep from throwing up on the pretty white carpet.

"You're pregnant?" she whispers, and I turn to see the look of hurt in her eyes. "How did that happen? I mean... when? Shit... I mean, why didn't you tell me?" She shakes her head, completely overwhelmed by the news.

"I don't know. I'm sorry; you know I love you," I whimper then look up at Z, and a surge of fury ignites my veins. "And you had no right to tell her, you big, fat jerk. I'm pregnant, not incapable of making my own fucking decisions." I stand up and shove past Z, whose glare softens when he sees my tears finally fall down my cheeks. "Fuck!" I scream when I get to the front door, when I realize I can't make my dramatic exit to really drive home the guilt he should feel for telling my best friend my secret before I got the chance to. "You have my keys. Either give them to me, or take me the fuck home."

I glance at July, my frown wobbling against my will

at the look on her face. She's never seen me like this, and Z doesn't even look a little bit fazed by my outburst.

Stupid, stupid, stupid! He was made for me. It's clear as day. And I put us through all this shit tonight for absolutely no reason. Fuck my life.

"I'm gonna head out," Sage says.

"Are you coming, or am I walking?" I raise a brow at Z, who grumbles something about his kitten having claws before he moves toward me. "I'll call you tomorrow," I tell July, my voice coming out breathier than I intended as Z's big form nears, and we walk out the door.

We don't say a word on our way back to our house.

Our house.

Fuck.

Again, what the hell is wrong with me?

What the fuck was I thinking, believing Z could possibly be cheating on me, when he just took me a week ago to meet his wonderful family? When we just found out I'm carrying his baby? When he just packed up all his stuff at the compound and moved in with me? Why am I so fucked up?

When we get home, I hop out of the car before he can come around and help me out, feeling jittery because I know we're going to have to talk this through. And I don't want to. I don't want to admit how freaking stupid I am. As soon as we're through the door though, I'm not given a chance to run from him. His big arms are scooping me up, and the next thing I know, he's cradling me in his lap as he sits down on the couch.

"What the hell were you thinking tonight, kitten?" he

whispers at the top of my head, kissing me there, and I can't help it as my body melts into his.

Suddenly, knowing I have to open up to him, I start to tremble before tears start falling in fat waves. And then comes the snot. And right behind that come the sobs. "I'm so freaking dumb, Z. So stupid. I don't know what's wrong with me! I... I... I... thought you were... were... *cheating on me!*" The last words come out as a loud wail, and LeFou howls inside his crate.

Z shushes him, and he immediately stops.

"What in the world, woman? Don't you know how much I love you? How much I worship the very ground you walk on?" he asks, and I can hear the hurt in his voice.

I cough out another sob. "I know! That's why I said I'm dumb! But... but you're so fucking secretive! When I ask you anything about your day, you always give me these vague answers. You never talk to me about what's going on with the club, which doesn't leave much else, because those guys were your life before I came along. So when you're me, and you've been cheated on in the past, that's automatically where my mind goes when you won't give me straight answers."

"That's what all this is about?" he asks, and he has the audacity to let out a laugh.

I glare up at him. "Yes, Z! That's what this is about. How can we have a good relationship if you aren't willing to communicate with me? Don't you trust me?"

He squeezes me tighter. "Of course I trust you, crazy girl. I wouldn't be here night after night, making love to you and *telling you* I love you, if I didn't trust you. I'm vague, because I'm trying to keep you safe. If you didn't know this about yourself, you like to take things into your own hands and go on these potentially dangerous adventures. If I tell you all that's going on, it would be just like you to plan something crazy, when I need you home, safe, protected, out of our way so we can handle it. Not to mention, you have my baby inside you now. So I didn't want to take any chance of you getting one of your bright ideas."

I have no sassy retort to that. He's exactly right.

Fuck.

But that still doesn't fix the fact he doesn't communicate with me.

I sniffle. My tears drying up the longer he rubs my back and soothes me with his reassurances. Finally, I concede, "What... what if I promised not to take matters into my own hands? Would you then promise to tell me things?"

His chocolate eyes stare into mine, and he must see I really need this for my peace of mind. "Against my better judgment, yes. If you swear on our child that you will not go on one of your adventures behind my back, then yes, I will always answer your questions. I won't be secretive anymore. I'll tell you everything that's going on. But you have to know I'm entrusting you with some fucking serious information, so I'm confiding in you, trusting that you won't tell anyone."

I flinch at that. "Not even July?" I wince.

He pooches out his lips, thinking for a moment. "Only after I clear with Wes that he's already told her."

"Deal." I sigh. I lay my head on his shoulder, letting his warmth seep into my skin, the nausea from earlier lessening the longer he holds me close. "So what's going on, Z? What was the secret meet-up about tonight?"

He moves us until he can pull out his phone from his pocket, and hides the screen from me as he says, "These pictures are graphic, kitten. Don't look unless you think you can handle it."

I nod, but I already know I'll look. It's just my nature.

He hands me his cell, and I gasp in shock.

It's an image of a woman not much older than me and July. She looks like she hasn't bathed in a long time, and her clothes are dirty. She's tied up, her nose bleeding, one eye swollen shut, black, and blue. There are also bruises on her arms in the shape of handprints.

"Mellissa Hornel. Twenty-five and a college graduate. She went missing three weeks ago. Had a date with a guy she met online. She never made it home, and three days later, she showed up for sale." He pauses. "Flip to the next one."

I do as he says, holding my breath. This girl is younger than Mellissa. Her blonde hair is tied up in a ponytail, her lip is swollen, and you can tell they tried to cover the bruise around her eye with makeup.

"Stacy Landon. She got a new boyfriend not knowing he's the son of a fucking piece of shit. Her parents filed a missing person report even though the police refused to believe she didn't run away. Her boyfriend's dad put her up for sale three days ago. Tonight, Wes was going to buy her. But our plan was... thwarted, as you say."

I look up at him. "Thwarted?" I squeak, dreading his response, because I know... I just *know*... I was the one who thwarted their carefully laid plans.

"There's nothing... *nothing*, kitten... that would keep

me from putting you first and foremost in my life. Not one thing. If I got a single hint that you're not safe, not where you're supposed to be, while I'm trying to take care of something, I'm going to drop everything I'm doing that second to make sure you're okay."

My lip trembles. "It's because of me that girl didn't get rescued tonight," I whimper.

His hold on me tightens. "We'll get another chance. We're not going to stop until we stop this fucker," he assures, and I nod against him, closing my eyes and eventually falling asleep in his arms.

14

KAYAN

"Fuuuu—fluke my life!" I growl at my cell, and Z chuckles. He doesn't understand why I've been trying to retrain myself to watch my language. It's not like we have a baby coming or anything. I side-eye him. "Stop laughing! It's another one."

And just like I knew he would, he stops once he knows who's calling. This is getting totally out of hand.

I told my parents our big news about a week ago. I had expected anger. I had expected their lectures and disappointment in me. I had expected and prepared myself for *all* the things.

Or so I thought.

What I hadn't expected was for my father to try to set me up with men he deemed worthy of our family.

Here I am, carrying the child of the man I love and who loves me, who I *live with,* and my father keeps giving out my phone number to random guys and telling them to ask me out.

And let's just say Z does not find it amusing.

At all.

So that's why I hold the phone away from him, where we're lying in bed, when he tries to reach for it. "No way! You are not answering. It's not their fault my dad is a completely messed-up douchebag. I don't want to make the poor guy pee himself. I just want the calls to stop," I whine.

He holds out his hand. "Kitten, give me the phone." When I still just shake my head, he says sincerely, "I promise I won't make him pee himself. I'll be nice and courteous."

I bite my lip, narrowing my eyes at him. He always keeps his promises, so I finally hand him my cell, watching as he slides his thumb across the screen to answer.

"Hello," he answers politely, his deep voice resonating throughout the bedroom. "Yes, this is Kayan's phone, not the wrong number." A pause. "Not your fault, Mark. Unfortunately, you've been lied to. Fortunately for us, Kayan and I are very happy in a committed relationship with our first child on the way."

My body breaks out in chills from head to toe at "*first* child," and my face goes soft as he keeps his calm tone.

"Yes. Oh, it's no problem. But would you mind doing me a solid? Because you're not the first to call, and it's upsetting my woman during her first trimester, and I'd like to keep her as calm as possible, since it's a delicate time during her pregnancy," he relays.

I can't help but smile. My man is addicted to googling all things pregnancy. He has thirteen—*thirteen!*—baby apps on his phone, and he religiously checks each and every one of them to see what's happening inside my uterus that day. If a giant, scary hot, former military biker can be adorable, then that's exactly what Z is. Freaking adorable.

"If it's not too much trouble, would you please spread it around your social circle that Kayan is taken and is glowingly, beautifully with child?"

I slap my hand across my face to hide the laughter that suddenly wants to burst from me. My whole body shakes from the suppressed cackles that want to break free. I move my hand, mouthing *With child?* And roll my eyes. God, I love this man.

He winks at me with a grin. "I'd greatly appreciate that, Mark. You have a great day." And he hangs up. "See? I told you I'd be nice."

I giggle. "That you did. I'm quite proud."

"Kitten, we've really gotta work on your bad habit of wanting to answer your phone while we're... busy," he says, kissing my inner thigh, where he's been lying between my legs, the backs of my thighs resting on his shoulders. "You're gonna give me a complex." He licks the place where my inner thigh connects to my center, making me squirm. "Make me think I'm not doing a good job down here, when you continue to pick it up every time it rings."

His tongue swipes from the very bottom of my opening to the hood over my clit, making me sigh. "No way, Z. There's no way you could be doing a *better* job. I swear—oooooh, just like that—it's just a compulsion. I'm an office manager—oh, God! I don't have it in me to not answer when the phone rings."

"Then new rule, kitten," he growls against my sensitive nub. "The phone goes on silent when we're in bed." He sucks my clit between his lips, and my eyes cross.

"Deal!" I cry, as shudders take over my entire body.

15

Z

"Yeah, so long story short, my best friend went and got herself kidnapped by these a-holes who were running a sex trafficking ring. Yep, the same guys who were fighting the dogs that were being dropped off at our clinic. Ugh. It's like she was trying to send me into early labor or something. Jeez. But of course, she's a badass. I mean a bad mamajama. I'd like to think it's all the adventures I've made her go on. My partner in crime put together all the skills I've taught her, and she not only saved herself, but a girl who had been taken before her. And the guys rode in on their motorcycles like knights on horses, and now they're both doing fine." Kayan bites a slice of orange, taking a sip of Sprite behind it. It's her go-to snack, a craving that points to our baby being a girl, according to my Glow Nurture app.

I watch as she continues to gossip on the phone with my mom, her feet propped up on the coffee table, the damn Chihuahua curled up at the top of her stomach between her tits.

"No shi— shut the front door. Seriously?" she corrects herself and I smile, both at her attempt to watch her language and at her sudden excitement. Her eyes meet mine. "Your mom just told me that espresso has less caffeine in it than regular brewed coffee. I can totally go back to having my lattes!"

I raise a brow and shake my head. "One a day, kitten. Doc said no more than one a day."

She sticks her bottom lip out, keeping her narrowed eyes on me as she then shoves two orange slices into her mouth. "Whatever."

After a few more minutes of chatting, Kayan hands me the phone, saying my mom wants to talk to me.

"Have you done it yet?" she asks, and my heart gives a heavy thud.

"Not yet, Ma," I reply, rubbing the back of my shaved head.

"Better get on it, son. Or some other guy is gonna come along and snatch her up right from under you," she teases, knowing about Kayan's dad trying to set her up with other men a couple months ago. My woman has formed a very strong bond with my mom, talks to her every day and tells her everything. It warms me like nothing else before. My mom has the daughter she always longed for, and Kayan has the parent she wished she'd had all along.

"I'm on it, Ma," I drawl. "Love you. And tell Pop I said hi."

"Will do, baby boy. Love you. Talk to you later," she replies, and we hang up.

I stand, taking Kayan's empty bowl and glass as I hand her back her cell. I dump the rinds in the trashcan, rinse the dishes and set them to the side of the sink, knowing she'll just want to reuse them in an hour or so, when the craving strikes again. I've lost count of how many bags of Cuties we've gone through. But she swears three tiny mandarins are what baby wants, not one big navel orange.

But whatever. What my kitten wants, my kitten gets.

I go over to the couch and hold out my hand to her, and she glances at it then up to my eyes. "Where we going? I just got comfy," she says, lifting her hand to pet LeFou.

"Just trust me on this one," I tell her, and she groans but holds onto the tiny dog before allowing me to help her up from her sprawled position on the couch. I take him from her, and she disappears into the bedroom to grab some shoes.

I put him in his crate, pausing to pat him on his little head. The little guy has grown on me. Hard not to like him when he listens to my every command and obviously seeks my approval, his entire body trembling as he tiptoes toward me when Kayan and I are relaxing. He'll look up at me with those watery bug-eyes, and I can just hear in his doggie voice, *"Please let me love you. Pick me up, Dad. I just want to snuggle."* In my head, he speaks in a weird accent, Spanish and French mixed together.

Kayan knew what she was doing when she started in with all the baby talk. *"LeFou wants hims daddy to hold him. Hold me, Daddy. I just want to lick every inch of your exposed skin. Don't make it weird. Just let it happen."*

When I look up from my kneeling position by the crate, I see Kayan grinning at me. "What?" I prompt.

She puts her hands behind her head and starts

circling her hips, singing "Big guy with a little dog. Big guy with a little dooooog." She sings it to match the way Chris Farley does in *Tommy Boy*, when he croons, "Fat guy in a little coat," and I can't help but chuckle. God, I love this woman more than anything.

I stand up and open the front door, swatting at her hand when she reaches for her purse hanging on one of the hooks I installed on the wall. I grab my bike keys, and hear her usual hesitation. "You sure it's a good idea—"

"How many times I gotta tell you, babe? Ain't no way I'd let anything happen to you. Plus, we'll be on back roads, so we won't have to worry about other vehicles either."

She looks at me curiously. "Back roads? Where are you taking me? Are you finally over me making fun of how much you love LeFou? Are you going to bury me somewhere so you can have him all to yourself?" she teases.

I just roll my eyes, locking the door behind us and listening to her jokes as she follows me to my bike.

"You should get him some little doggy goggles and a scarf, and put a basket on the front of your bike for him to ride in," she continues, swinging her leg over as she gets on behind me. "I'd say a side car, but he's only four pounds. A basket on the front would be plenty. And I'll even get you some pretty streamers to come out of your handlebars!"

That pulls me out of my nervous quiet, and I snort out a laugh before starting the bike, the engine roaring to life and making Kayan sigh in my ear as she wraps herself around my back. As weary as she was in the beginning, she loves to take rides now, even if she is a little hesitant about doing it pregnant. But she's barely showing yet, and I've always been a safe rider. It's why I got a Harley instead of a crotch rocket. I'm not about speed and splitting lanes. I just like to cruise.

We're at the destination in half an hour, and as I hold the bike steady for Kayan to climb off first, she comes around to the front, looks behind her at the building, and then back at me, raising an eyebrow and one side of her top lip.

"Um, babe. I appreciate the thought, but bar food isn't on my list of cravings. Plus, I thought you said I wasn't allowed to come back here ever again," she says, and I chuckle, getting off the bike and immediately towering over her. "Also, I think they're closed. Or they're just really, really dead." She glances around at the empty parking lot.

"One, Momma's Country is a safe place again, now that we helped the kid and his dad get out from under Snake's guys. It's now under the protection of The Broken Eagle Motorcycle Club, thanks to two crazy girls in catsuits." I smile, and she beams up at me proudly. "Two, they're closed until tonight. But they happen to have delicious chicken wings and burgers, so don't knock 'em till you try 'em."

She giggles. "Fair enough. We'd have to eat out on the patio though. Too much smoke inside." Her hands unconsciously go to her little belly as she glances back at the bar. But my voice pulls her back.

"Three." I reach into my pocket and pull out the ring I have waiting there. I picked it out a month ago, but have been trying to wait for the perfect moment to ask her. I go down on my knee, next to my bike and in front of the woman I love, who lets out a squeak as I reach out to pull her hands from her belly to hold in my left palm, the ring ready for her finger in my right. It never fails to stand out how tiny she is compared to me. "It was here, at this bar, that I first laid eyes on you. You were on one of your adventures, dressed in a catsuit in the middle of a country bar, and all eyes, including mine, were on you. I thought, *Who is this delicious feline, this sexy little Cat Woman?* But when I spoke to you, you tried to skitter away like a scared kitten. And that's when I started calling you just that—my kitten. But you proved over and over again that my kitten has claws, and even though it first intrigued me how shy you were—it was in this exact parking spot that I told you I'd never had shy in my bed before—it was when you'd bare those claws and sharp fangs that really made me want to make you mine."

Tears start to fall down her cheeks, and for once, it doesn't make me crazy. I know these are happy tears because of the smile stretched across her beautiful face.

"I love every single one of your facets, Kayan. I love your shyness, and your sassiness. I love how feisty you can be, and how loyal you are to your best friend. I love how you give me shit, and can take it all the same. And I want you to know that it's not because you're pregnant that I want to make you mine forever. Our baby is just the cherry on top, even though I don't even deserve the cake in the first place."

She pulls her hand from mine to cup my cheek at that, seeing the emotion on my face. "There's no man *more* deserving than you, Z." She sniffles.

I shake my head with a smile, my nose prickling. "The first decade of my life, my parents made me believe I was the least deserving person on the planet. I was lucky, so fucking lucky, to then be adopted by two of the most loving people in this world, but I can't help but fear it's still in me somewhere that I'll turn out like my biological mom and dad. How strong is nature? Is it in my blood? Am I going to be a horrible father and husband?" I finally voice my fears.

She shakes her head frantically, her tears showering my face, cleansing me of my doubts. "No, no way. Because you know what? Louisa is your blood too, and like you said, she is one of the most loving, kind, generous, and nurturing people I've ever met. I have no doubt it's your nature to take after her and Mateo. You are too good to me, too protective and over-the-top loving to make me have even a shadow of a doubt. This baby is going to be the luckiest kid in the world to have you as their daddy. And I'll hit the jackpot... if you ever get around to actually proposing. Isn't your knee starting to hurt by now, kneeling on that gravel, babe?" She tilts her head, and I can't help the bark of laughter that erupts from my chest.

This woman. This crazy, beautiful, perfect woman.

"Kayan, my kitten. Would you make me the luckiest bastard in the world and be my wife?" I ask.

She juts out a sassy hip and puts her right hand on it, scolding me, "How many times do I gotta tell you to watch your language in front of our baby?" But then she grins wide as she threads her left ring finger through the ring before wrapping her arms around my neck, kissing me on top of my head the way Mom does to Dad. But unlike the Amazon my mom is, Kayan is so small that she's barely taller than me while I'm on my knee.

Which, now that she mentioned it, is starting to ache a little.

So I stand with her still wrapped around me, pulling her off her feet as I circle my arms around her waist, feeing her little bump fit against my chest as her legs come to lock around me. She laughs up at the sky as I spin her around, and then her lips come down on mine, kissing me like I'm the very air she needs to breathe.

When she finally pulls back, she says, "That's a yes, by the way," and I smile.

"Oh, good. Now, let's get you home so I can consummate our engagement," I tease, turning to set her perfect ass on the back of my bike.

"I don't think that's a thing. But..." She rubs her belly, her little tongue poking out the side of her mouth as she thinks. "I do wonder what it'd be like to suck orange juice off your cock. You think it'd be as hot as the chocolate syrup we tried at Club Alias?"

I go rock-hard instantly inside my jeans, adjusting myself as I lift my leg to get on the bike. "Kitten, I think you sucking anything off my cock would be hot."

And I chuckle as she adds right before my pipes roar to life, "Bo-Berry Biscuit frosting. Oh my Goooood, yes."

The End

Turn the page for a special note from the author!

NOTE FROM THE AUTHOR

I hope you enjoyed Kayan and Z's happily ever after! If you'd like to learn more about my Club Alias Series, book 1 is the *Confession Duet*, which is Z's friend Corbin's story with his Vi. You can read it as a complete boxed set (*Confession Duet*) for a special price, or as two separate books (*Before the Lie* and *Truth Revealed*). But trust me, you won't want to read *BTL* without having *TR* handy to start right after you finish. That cliffy is BRUTAL (hehe!).

For those of you who have not read Aurora Rose Reynold's *Until July*, Z and Kayan are the hero and heroine's best friends. I definitely recommend this funny, hot, and exciting tale of the feisty vet and her yummy biker. Plus, if you fell in love with Z and Kayan, you'll get to see where they originated, and why I chose to write their love story.

CLUB ALIAS SERIES (Available in KU)
    Book 1/ *Confession Duet Boxed Set (Corbin and Vi's Story)*

Book 2/ *Seven: A Club Alias Novel*
Book 2.5/ *Mission: Accomplished Novella Boxed Set*
Book 3/ *Knight: A Club Alias Novel*

ABOUT THE AUTHOR

KD Robichaux wanted to be a romance author since the first time she picked up her mom's Sandra Brown books at the ripe old age of twelve. She went to college to become a writer, but then married and had babies. Putting her dream job on hold to raise her family as a stay at home mom, who read entirely too much, she created a blog where she could keep her family and friends up-to-date on all the hottest reads. From there, by word of mouth, her blog took off and she began using her hard-earned degree as a Senior Editor for Hot Tree Editing. When her kids started school, and with the encouragement from her many author friends, she finally sat down and started working on her first series, The Blogger Diaries, her very own real life romance.

Join my Reader Group: https://www.facebook.com/groups/KDRobsMob/

Join my Newsletter: https://mailchi.mp/afd29557f6e1/join-kd-robichauxs-newsletter

Like my blog page: https://www.facebook.com/MessyBunBookBlog/

Check out my website: https://authorkdrobichaux.wixsite.com/authorkdrobichaux

facebook.com/authorkdrobichaux

twitter.com/Kaylathebiblio

instagram.com/kaylathebibliophile

amazon.com/author/kdrobichaux

bookbub.com/authors/kd-robichaux

pinterest.com/authorkdrobicha

goodreads.com/KDRobichaux